For Joe P, Joe H, Jacob,
Josh, Sam and Billy

ORCHARD BOOKS
338 Euston Road, London NW1 3BH
Orchard Books Australia
Level 17/207 Kent Street, Sydney, NSW 2000

A paperback original
First published in 2011

ISBN 978 1 40831 208 7

Text © Rose Impey 2011
Cover illustrations © Andy Smith 2011
Inside illustrations by Steve Sims © Orchard Books 2011

A CIP catalogue record for this book is available
from the British Library.

1 3 5 7 9 10 8 6 4 2 (hardback)
1 3 5 7 9 10 8 6 4 2 (paperback)

Printed in Great Britain

Orchard Books is a division of Hachette Children's Books,
an Hachette UK company.

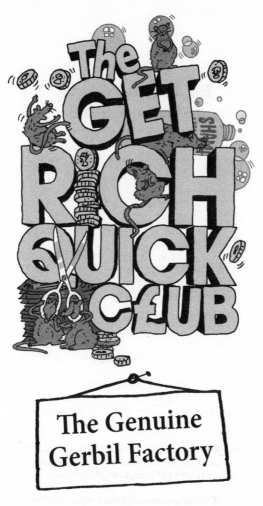

The GET RICH QUICK CLUB

The Genuine Gerbil Factory

Rose Impey

ORCHARD

CHAPTER ONE

This is your lucky day.

You *lucky person* have been chosen to join the soon-to-be-world-famous *Get Rich Quick Club*.

And I'm Robin Banks. *Yeah, yeah,* spare me the joke – it's so old it's practically got mould on it.

Although, to be honest, robbing banks is one of the few crazy things we haven't tried so far. But, as I'm always telling Baxter: if you want to be a millionaire, you've got to start somewhere. It's like the lottery, *you've got to be in it to win it.*

Right?

That's Baxter on the left. Ugly devil, isn't he?
Only joking – we're best mates really. Whatever
you do, don't call him Billy. Only his mum does
that. *Everyone else* calls him Baxter. Or, if he's
being a real poser, which is most of the time, he
likes to be called *The Dude*!

That's me, the good-looking one on the right –
just kidding again.

You can call me Banksy. Sometimes I'm Robo, or Blue-ey, but more of that later.

And this – *da daa* – is our clubhouse, the nerve centre of the *Get Rich Quick Club*, or GRQC for short. Don't worry about the *Members Only* bit. Like I said, we're making an exception for you.

But, before we go inside, there's a couple of things I should warn you about.

Number 1: *the smell.* What can I say - it's rank. And here's the reason why: this little weed is Baxter's kid brother, Sam. Don't get me wrong, it's not *him* that smells, it's his *menagerie.* Right from the beginning, the club was my idea, but the shed belongs to Baxter's dad. That means we have to share it with Sam, who's only six but already pretty weird.

Sam's an animal freak – potty about anything with four legs, wings or a tail, so the shed smells like a zoo on a hot day. Not to mention the other gross stuff he collects.

I'll bet no other millionaires started out surrounded by animal poo and sheep's eyeballs. I'll bet Alan Sugar didn't. That's *Lord* Sugar, my all-time hero. Do you know how much he's worth? *Over seven billion pounds*! That's *seriously* rich. One day I'm going to be his apprentice, then look out!

Oh, and number 2...

As well as Stinky Sam, I should also mention the Dreaded Dingdong. Real name: Annabelle. Get it? She's in the same class as Baxter and me,

which means we're stuck with her at school and lumbered with her at home. That's because she's Baxter's cousin and lives on the farm next door. So I suppose it's partly her shed as well.

Actually, Dingdong's not that bad, but *don't* tell her I said so. To be honest, both of them come in useful sometimes.

For example: Sam's such a little squirt, we can squeeze him into all sorts of places like half-open windows, through holes in fences... down toilets... No, no, that last one's a joke. Honest. We've never put Sam down a toilet! Not so far, anyway!

And don't look so worried, we're not *really* into breaking and entering...unless it's *absolutely* necessary. But, if it is, we sometimes need a look-out, which is where Dingdong comes in.

Take our last business venture – Baxter and me would've been seriously struggling without them.

Who else but Sam would have fitted through a cat-flap? And no one but Dingdong could have kept the old lady happy all afternoon like that. *I know, I know*, Dingdong could probably talk the back leg off a deaf donkey, which usually drives us crazy, but that day it came in very useful.

And let's get this quite clear from the start: we weren't actually *stealing* anything – more sort of… *borrowing*. We always intended to put the gerbil back…after we'd used it. But you know what they say about the best laid plans.

Come on, let's go in and I'll tell you all about it.

Take a deep breath and hold your nose; you'll soon get used to it. No, I'm lying. You probably won't, but at least you won't notice when Baxter trumps. Baxter's trumps are almost as bad as his sense of humour. And when I say that's bad I mean *bad*! It's the main reason he's my best mate – well, that and the shed.

So this is where it all happens. See that desk? That's our conference table, and we've each got a chair. You'll notice Baxter's swivels and mine doesn't – but as he *always* reminds me: *It is his shed!*

So grab yourself a Jammy Dodger and park your bottom. Then I'll let you in on some of my top secrets for a successful business.

Ready? OK. Number 1: *Ideas! Ideas! Ideas!*

It's the most important thing, to come up with a really epic money-making idea. You know, one that's got legs.

And, to be honest, *The Genuine Gerbil Factory* looked like it had legs – and some to spare. In fact it looked like a sure-fire, gold-plated, number-one winner – at least to begin with.

CHAPTER TWO

It all started like this: It was a Saturday morning and Baxter was sharpening the end of a long stick with his Swiss Army knife. He was in full camo gear as usual and he had his boots up on the desk. That really ticks me off. It's not exactly business-like. I mean, you wouldn't see Lord Sugar doing that. But there's no point saying anything because – *yeah, yeah, it is his shed*!

I'd just finished counting the readies, which didn't take long. We weren't exactly close to our first million.

"*Four pounds fifty-five!*" Baxter said in disgust. "How can it be that low?"

"Because last month," I reminded him, "we had to fork out for a new motor for your mum's vacuum cleaner."

A few weeks before we'd launched our new house cleaning business – *Who you gonna call? Dustbunnies.* I can promise you that name didn't get *my* vote! But it was still a really mint idea that didn't go *quite* to plan.

And then there was the fall out from our next venture: dog walking and other pet services. Let's not even go there right now.

"We need a new business plan," I said.

Baxter looked thoughtful but kept whittling away at his bit of wood. He already had a lethal-looking spike in his hand but he kept on as the stick got shorter and shorter. Baxter loves – and I mean *loves* – destroying stuff.

I suppose everybody does. But it's pretty well Baxter's favourite thing in the world.

Sam was there, as usual, sitting on the floor holding two gerbils together like he was trying to persuade them to mate. You could tell they weren't happy about it. Their little legs were pedalling away in thin air like cartoon mice trying to escape from the cat.

All round him there was a growing pile of droppings on the floor adding to the stink in

the place. It was just the three of us so far. On Saturday mornings Dingdong's always at her ballet class.

But, speak of the devil, suddenly there she was, hammering on the door and yelling, "If you've got Leonardo de Caprio in there, Sam, you're dead meat." The door handle rattled, then she banged again, yelling even louder, "You'd better let me in, or else!"

It was obvious who it was, but Baxter still called back, "You know the secret knock."

Dingdong gave one long bang, three short raps, and another long one.

"*And* the pin number," Baxter yelled.

(It's instead of a password; that was my idea.)

She rattled it off, through gritted teeth. Finally, Baxter nodded for me to let her in.

As soon as I opened the door Dingdong flew through it like a jet-propelled missile. She almost flattened me behind it. Then she pounced on Sam and grabbed her gerbil back. She hugged it so tight I expected the poor creature to snuff it.

"I was only *borrowing* him," Sam whined.

Dingdong narrowed her eyes at Sam.

"I was practising…" he added.

"*Practising…*" she almost snarled, "*on Leonardo!*"

"Just until I get a female." Sam eyed the small pile of money on the desk. "Lend us a tenner, Baxter," he begged, "so I can get one."

"A tenner, just for a smelly fur-ball?" Baxter laughed. "In your dreams."

"Oh, hold on one minute," I said, turning to Sam. "Are you trying to tell us one little gerbil costs a *tenner*?"

"Females do," he said, "they're dearer."

"Well, they would be, wouldn't they?" Dingdong said, smugly, but no one paid any attention. Baxter and me were far too busy doing sums in our heads. I could almost see little £ signs flashing across his eyeballs.

"How many gerbils in a litter?" he asked Sam.

"Five? Maybe six?"

"If half those gerbils were girls…" Baxter said, thinking aloud.

"We could soon have three breeding pairs…" I said, finishing his sentence.

"Yeah, but they might not be," Dingdong interrupted.

"And if each pair had five…or six babies…"
Baxter continued, ignoring her.

"Three sixes are eighteen," I said, before he'd
even got his calculator out of the drawer.

"And, just say, half those babies had *six*
babies…" he went on.

We were both getting really excited now. It was
like a footie match. Baxter and me were steaming
down the wing passing the ball between us with
nobody in our way.

"*And half those babies had six babies…*"
I added, giving it another nifty kick.

"They probably won't, though," Dingdong said,
trying again to intercept. But we ploughed right
through her.

"*And half those babies had six babies!*" Baxter's
voice rose as he prepared to shoot.

"In no time we'd have a *million* gerbils!"
I punched the air.

"*Result!*" we both yelled, as we jumped out of our chairs and hugged like we'd just scored for Man U.

We'd clearly left Sam and Dingdong somewhere down the other end of the pitch. They looked at us as if we'd finally flipped.

OK, I know…we're not stupid. We realised things might not work out *quite* that smoothly. But the numbers were looking impressive. And like I always say: *you can't argue with the numbers.*

Baxter spread his arms wide and brought the other two up to speed, "Welcome to the Genuine Gerbil Factory," he said, grinning.

"Neat title," I nodded. Baxter and me like a bit of alliteration.

And that brings me to Number 2 of my top secrets for success: *It's all in the name.* It doesn't matter how good your idea is, if you don't have a catchy business title, you're dead in the water. Right?

"A gerbil factory!" Sam said, suddenly cheering up. He looked like his biggest dream had just come true. But Dingdong *wasn't* sold on the idea. She clutched Leonardo to her like we'd just announced the opening of a gerbil-pie-making factory. And

Leonardo was going in the first pie!

"This'll all end in tears," she told us. "And when it does, don't anybody say I didn't warn you."

"*Yeah, yeah,*" we said, pretending to yawn.

As a matter of principle, we try *never* to let Dingdong have the last word, but, as usual, she got it.

"And another thing…" she said.

CHAPTER THREE

"**F**or starters, you still don't have a female…" Dingdong pointed out, determined to bring us back to earth.

True, we had Sam's gerbil: The Terminator – don't even ask – and Leonardo Di Caprio, but no female.

"And you don't have a tenner to buy one," she added. To be accurate we didn't even have half a tenner.

Baxter went on whittling, while I tried to move things on.

"OK, let's eliminate the obvious," I said. "Anyone got a birthday coming up?"

Everyone shook their heads.

"Anyone got any pocket money we can tap?"

Ditto. Dingdong sometimes has, because she saves up – for useless things like ballet shoes – but not this time.

"Can't we just borrow one?" Baxter suggested. "The school gerbil is a girl, isn't she?"

"Genius," I said. The name Dotty's a bit of a giveaway!

But Sam, who seems to know these things, told us, "You'd need to keep her for at least five weeks.

You can't take babies away from the mother the minute they're born, you know."

"Miss Waites wouldn't leave Dotty with you lot for five *minutes*, never mind five weeks!" Dingdong laughed. "Not on this planet, no way."

Dingdong might be a bit of a know-it-all but on this occasion she was probably right.

"There must be *someone* who'd lend us a gerbil," I said. I looked hopefully at the four pounds fifty-five. "Or sell us one *very cheap*."

Sam suddenly jumped up, bouncing from foot to foot, like he needed a wee. "Mrs Gumboil!" he said.

We all looked at him, waiting for some explanation.

"*Mrs Gumboil*," he repeated. "She's got gerbils, loads of them."

Mrs Gumboil is an old lady whose house is on our way to school. We don't know her real name, but we call her that because she's always sucking big sweets.

Sam said he once peered in her window and saw loads of gerbils – cages of them, *he said*. But Sam's like Baxter: you never know what to believe.

"What would an old lady be doing with loads of gerbils?" I asked, suspiciously.

"Probably eats them," Baxter grinned. He puffed out his cheeks, then made a gobbling noise. He finished with a loud, disgusting burp. Baxter does seriously epic burps.

"Maybe that's what she's always *sucking* on," I said, grinning back.

"Ugh! *Nobody* eats gerbils," Dingdong said, disgusted.

"Baxter probably would," I said.

Baxter nodded. "I might," he agreed, "if it was a matter of life and death – slugs, beetles, cockroaches, earwigs...anything."

Dingdong looked as if she might throw up. "You are totally disgusting," she told him.

Baxter grinned. He likes to think he's Ray Mears. He claims he could survive indefinitely in the wild with only his penknife and a length of frayed rope. Personally I'd give him ten minutes – wait, make that five.

But we needed to get back to the subject.

"If she's got loads of gerbils," I said, "she might sell us one. And she might be cheaper than the pet shop." I stuffed our money into my pocket and stood up. "Come on, let's go."

One of my mottoes is: *If you're going to do it; do it NOW!*

You know, like unloading the dishwasher, or cutting your toenails, or doing that boring bit of English homework. The job's not going to go away, so you might just as well get on with it.

But Baxter has the opposite approach. His

could be summed up as: *whatever it is put it off for as long as you can – and even then try to wriggle out of it.*

"What, *now?*" he moaned. "It's nearly lunchtime."

Some survival expert!

But Sam was already at the door, carrying The Terminator in a small cage as if there wasn't a moment to lose in finding him a mate. Even Dingdong was on her feet, tucking Leonardo di Caprio inside her trackie top.

"The sooner we get it done," I pointed out, "the sooner we make our first million."

Baxter reluctantly dragged himself out of his seat. He pulled his cap to a more serious angle and tied his precious rope around his waist. "OK, team!" he said, decisively, "let's do this," as if the whole thing had been his idea in the first place and the rest of us were just a bunch of slackers.

He's such a poser!

We locked the shed and set off. Baxter led the way as if it was an outward-bound expedition. But I noticed when we reached the old lady's house he dropped back and waited for everyone to catch up. Then they all stood looking at me.

"Now what?" said Dingdong.

I shrugged. It was hardly rocket science. "We knock on the door and ask if we can buy one of her gerbils." Of course, when I say *we*…you can guess who that meant.

"Yeah, go for it, Blue-ey," said Baxter, leaning against the gate-post and starting to whittle again.

Let me explain where that nickname comes from.

I don't know what kind of a kid you are, but I'm just ordinary. I'm not a nerd or a geek, whatever Baxter might tell you. Ordinary for me means living with my mum – just the two of us – no dad, no brothers, no sisters. No pets!

Ordinary for Baxter means being one of a great big noisy tribe. There's him and Sam and their older brother, Wayne, their mum, Carol, their dad, Keith, and the baby, Clara. Or The Trump-Machine as Baxter calls her. "No kidding," he says, "sometimes it's so loud she wakes herself up." Plus loads of dogs and puppies.

So his mum's far too busy to notice whether Baxter cleans his teeth – he doesn't – or does his

homework – *never* – or changes his underpants –
what do you think?

But my mum notices *everything*: so I reckon
it's just easier to do stuff like putting the toilet seat
down and saying please and thank you.

The trouble is I never hear the end of it from
Baxter.

"Who's a blue-eyed boy?" he goes on. "Who's
a real PP?" Which in case you don't know means
Parent-Pleaser.

So it is a bit of a no brainer: if anyone was
likely to get on the right side of a grownup, it
was going to be yours truly!

I stepped through the gate and knocked
on the door. It's cool, I thought. This'll be
a bit of a breeze.

But guess what?

CHAPTER FOUR

We tried the bell first, then the doorknocker – several times. But there was no answer. We'd been there all of two minutes before Baxter was moaning: "I'm hungry. Let's go home. We can come back some other time."

"She might be deaf," Dingdong said, ignoring him. "You should try again."

So I tried again. This time I made such a racket Baxter said, "She'd have to be *dead* never mind deaf not to hear that."

"What if she is?" said Dingdong. "You hear

about old people dying and no one knowing."

"Yeah," Baxter nodded. "Lying there rotting for six months, eaten by maggots."

Dingdong rolled her eyes and did that *tutting* thing she does.

I thought they were both being stupid. But I had to admit the house did look pretty empty and neglected. The curtains in the front room were closed. There was a paper sticking out of the letterbox and milk bottles on the step.

"She's probably on holiday," I said.

Sam put down his gerbil and walked up to the letterbox. He pulled out the paper and peeped through the flap, which was just about his height.

"You can't do that," Dingdong gasped, but Sam already had.

"*Wow!*" he whispered.

When he turned to face us, Sam spread his hands like a magician demonstrating a particularly simple trick. "You want gerbils?" he said. "Well, take a look in there."

Although it felt a bit risky, we took it in turns to peep through the flap. Any minute I expected the old lady to walk downstairs and find a pair of eyes staring at her through her own letterbox – giving her a heart attack!

For once, Sam wasn't exaggerating. When I say the place was stuffed with gerbils, I mean it was *stuffed*. Most of them were in cages or tanks but

you could see some just running around like it
was a holiday camp for gerbils.

"Oh, *yes!*" Baxter hissed. "There's no way she's
going to miss one of those."

"Even if we could get in, which we can't,"
Dingdong pointed out, "you can't just steal one."

"It wouldn't be stealing," Baxter insisted. "We'd
bring it back after it's had its babies. We'd just be
borrowing it."

We should have listened to Baxter, instead
of standing around arguing, wrestling with our

consciences. In no time we'd have been swimming in gerbils and rolling in money.

But we didn't – we *ummed and erred* instead.

That's when everything took a completely different turn. That's when Dingdong looked up and saw *the hand at the bedroom window*.

If I hadn't seen it myself, I'd have sworn she'd made it up. But it was *definitely* a hand – and it *did* look as if it was waving.

"Come on," said Dingdong. "We've got to go and see what she wants."

The rest of us were more in favour of legging it, but she gave us one of those looks. You know, like your mum gives you. Like she's letting you know she's *really disappointed* with you.

"OK, OK," I growled. "Just for two minutes."

We all turned back – even Baxter and his bloomin' stomach.

"This had better be good," he said.

"She obviously needs us," said Dingdong.

The way I looked at it: if she *obviously needed* us she'd have come down and let us in. But she didn't, even though we waited – for at least three minutes. So then we went round trying every window and every door. In the end, the only option left was the cat flap.

We had to push Sam quite hard to get him through.

"Owww! That's my head!" he complained.

But we managed and in no time we could hear him on the other side sounding like he was climbing the stairway to heaven. "Oh, oh, *megawow*!" he moaned.

"What's going on?" Baxter shouted.

Sam poked his nose back through the cat flap.

"It's mental, Baxter. There's loads more in the kitchen," he almost cried with joy. "They're *everywhere*."

"Just open the *bloomin'* door," Baxter told him, "and let us in."

The first thing I noticed when we got inside was the familiar smell. The old lady's kitchen smelt just like our shed – actually, even worse than our shed.

The whole kitchen seemed to be alive. There were cages full of gerbils balanced on every surface: on top of the fridge, the washing machine, the breakfast bar. There was even a pair in a salad spinner on the cooker top. There was one looking rather poorly in a goldfish bowl and a couple under the kitchen table that had gone beyond poorly. Sam wrapped them gently in old newspaper and disposed of them in the kitchen bin.

The twittering and squeaking was almost as bad as the smell. It was an absolute madhouse and I couldn't wait to get out of there. "OK," I said desperately, "we need a plan."

"Who needs a plan?" Baxter said, scooping up

a gerbil in each hand. "We've got what we came for, let's beat it now."

"We are *not* going to steal them," Dingdong said again.

I agreed that didn't seem right. "Why don't we leave the four pound fifty-five on the kitchen table?" I said, taking it out of my pocket. "We'd be doing the old lady a favour. She's clearly got more gerbils than she can handle."

"But what about *her*?" Dingdong said. "What if she's ill? What if she's *dying*?" she added dramatically.

For a minute I'd forgotten that was the reason we'd sort of broken in. Even then I could still have

persuaded myself the house was empty.

"Maybe we *imagined* a hand," I said. "Maybe it was…a bit of curtain blowing about."

Yeah, yeah, not very convincing, I know. But I'd have settled for it – if we hadn't heard the bang. It suddenly sounded as if *someone* was banging on the bedroom floor with a big wooden stick. We just about jumped out of our skins.

"Pretty noisy those curtains," Dingdong said, sarcastically.

We all looked at each other. Baxter was already half way out of the door. And to be honest, we could still have legged it – taking a couple of gerbils with us – but somehow I just couldn't. I did the same thing all over again: I *dithered*. And this time I only had myself to blame.

CHAPTER FIVE

I really didn't *mean* to, but I found myself saying, "We should probably check she's OK. You know…just in case."

Baxter raised his hands. "Don't look at me. I'm not going up there." Then he added darkly, "You never know what she might do."

Images of the old witch in Hansel and Gretel, fattening us up to make little boy pie, flitted through my head.

But everyone was looking my way again as if *we* meant *me*, as usual. Not this time. No way, José.

"I think Dingdong should go up," I said.

Dingdong looked horrified. "Why me?"

"I agree," said Baxter. Sam raised his hand as if it was an official vote.

"Suppose she's ill in bed," I said. "It might frighten her if one of us suddenly appears round the door."

"A girl'd be less scary," Baxter agreed.

"Definitely," Sam nodded, closing the deal.

"Less scary than your ugly mugs, for sure," Dingdong conceded. "But I'm not going on my own."

"I'll wait at the bottom of the stairs," I promised. "If I hear you scream, I'll come up."

"Oh, very comforting," she said, still standing there. But we kept on staring at her until we'd worn her down.

"*All right*," she snapped, passing me Leonardo to hold. "But if you leave me here on my own," she warned us, "you're all dead meat! Understand?"

We all nodded; we believed her. Dingdong can be pretty scary.

I followed her into the hall, slipping Leonardo in my right-hand jacket pocket. I watched her climb the stairs and try a couple of doors before she found the right room. I waited a minute or two but when there was no scream I turned back to the kitchen.

Along the walls there were more cages stacked precariously. The slightest nudge could have sent them crashing to the floor, letting loose even more animals. One escapee ran along a radiator top. Another inquisitive creature on a high shelf lost its balance and fell to a certain death. Or it would have, if I hadn't been there to make a brilliant save. I tucked it in my other jacket pocket for safe-keeping. Well, it did owe me its life!

Through an open door, I saw a downstairs bathroom. There were more tanks and cages, piled high in the bath. At a quick count there were twenty-five containers just in that room.

There was suddenly shouting coming from the kitchen. I hurried back there to find Baxter, the great white hunter, hopping from foot to foot like he'd got killer ants in his pants.

"Don't stand there grinning," he shouted, still dancing around. It seemed some brave – or very stupid – gerbil had shot up his trouser leg. "Help me get it out."

"No way," I snorted. "You're on your own, *Dude.*"

I quickly followed Sam's example, tucking my own jeans into my socks to make sure the same thing didn't happen to me.

Baxter went on hopping about until common sense returned. He finally sat down, trapping the gerbil under his hand and carefully squeezing it down his leg. When its tail poked out round his ankle Baxter made a grab for it.

"Got you, you little rodent," he said through gritted teeth. But he hadn't. The gerbil sank its teeth into his thumb then made its escape, under the washing machine.

"That'll teach you," Baxter shouted triumphantly after it, as if he somehow thought he'd won.

All this time, Sam was sitting quietly on the floor surrounded by cages of gerbils, trying to sort the males from the females. He didn't seem a bit bothered when one or two ran up his back and over his head.

It gave me the creeps. I couldn't help wondering how the place had ever got this bad. I knew my mum would seriously freak out if she saw it. To be honest, I couldn't wait to get out of there.

But we really couldn't go without Dingdong so I thought I might as well join in the fun. Baxter was charging about the kitchen clutching a plastic soup bowl, slamming it down over anything that moved. As revenge for his bleeding thumb, he was determined to catch every last one of the runaways.

"Geronimo!" he yelled, advancing on the poor creatures, almost scaring them to death.

I found a plastic sieve and joined him, waving it and yelling, "Prepare to be sieved!"

When we ran out of containers to put them in, I tucked a couple more in my pockets. I tried to keep the males in the right and females in the left. But, to be honest, I hadn't much idea which was which, so it was mostly guess work. I just had to hope there wasn't enough room for any hanky-panky.

After a few minutes Baxter had given up the chase and was sitting crunching on something. "Want some?" he offered, holding out an open packet of spaghetti he'd found in a cupboard.

I shook my head. I don't generally eat raw pasta.

"I've had worse," Baxter said, "You know, in the jungle…"

"Yeah, yeah," I cut him off. "I know…you'd eat your own feet if you were hungry enough."

He looked for a moment as if he was seriously considering the possibility.

By now even *my* stomach was beginning to grumble and no wonder. When I looked at my watch it was gone two o'clock! I'd never been so relieved to hear Dingdong's fairy footsteps clomping down the stairs.

Finally we could get out of this place. And, I'd decided, we were taking at least a pair of gerbils with us. I wasn't so desperate that I'd lost sight of why we'd come in the first place.

By the way, that's another of my business tips – *always keep your goal in sight*. You'll find it works for football too.

Dingdong strolled into the kitchen. She didn't look like someone who'd had a close call with a witch. But whatever had happened upstairs she was in no hurry to tell *us* about it.

"Well?!" I asked, gesturing that we might like some information before the next millennium.

"It's like I said," she told us, smugly, "she's had a fall and broken her ankle."

"How do you know it's broken?" I asked, suspiciously. Dingdong *is* related to the Baxters, after all.

"Well, she can't get downstairs," she said. "She can hardly get out of bed."

"Did you ask her about the gerbils?" Sam said, more urgently.

Dingdong rolled her eyes. "I think she's a bit…" she circled her finger to indicate the old lady might not be quite with it.

"How long do you think she's been up there?" I asked.

Dingdong shrugged. "She doesn't seem to know what day it is."

This was the point where I began to realise we'd got ourselves into something we probably weren't up to dealing with.

"You've been up there all this time," Baxter complained, "and you've found out next to nothing."

"Oh, she'd like something to eat," Dingdong suddenly remembered. "She's very hungry."

"What?!" I couldn't believe my ears.

"Well, when I asked if we could have one of her gerbils, she said: you can have *anything*, my dear, if you'll get me a piece of toast and a cup of tea."

"We haven't got time for that," I said.

"But it could be *days* since she ate anything proper," Dingdong said, dramatically. "She's only had sweets to keep her alive."

I looked round the kitchen. There was nothing obviously edible in sight. The bread bin was empty. In the fridge there were a few things that looked like they'd walk out on their own given the chance.

"What are we going to do?" Dingdong asked me.

It was times like this I wished I could be more like Baxter; he'd have gone, scarpered. And, believe me, I wanted to, but I just can't help being...*responsible*!

I looked at the money on the table and groaned. One of us would have to go and buy a loaf. But then I had a brainwave. My mum always keeps frozen sliced bread in the freezer. Sure enough, when I looked, so did the old lady.

"Defrost some of this and make her some toast," I told Dingdong. "Put the kettle on," I told Baxter.

Can you believe, he had the cheek to ask *me* what *my* last servant died of?! But I ignored him and organised a plate and a cup, then searched in the cupboard for some long-life milk.

"If it's that long since the old lady had anything to eat," Sam muttered, "it must be a long time since the gerbils were fed."

"Never mind the bloomin' gerbils," Baxter complained, "it's hours since my breakfast. I'll have some of that toast," he told Dingdong.

"You can get in line," she snapped. "We're all hungry, you know."

I suddenly flipped and told them both to *shut up*. "And as soon as you've given her the toast…" I said.

"And tea," Dingdong added.

"…*whatever*," I said, "we're leaving."

"Good," said Baxter, picking up a couple of gerbils for a fast getaway.

Dingdong was spreading two pieces of toast with some very old-looking butter she'd found on the table. "But we can't just leave her," she said. "She's scared social services will put her in an old people's home. They did that to my nan's next door neighbour, you know."

I thought the old lady was right. They probably

would if they saw the state of this place.

"Not our problem," said Baxter in his usual caring-sharing way.

"What if we just got the place a bit cleaned up?" Dingdong suggested hopefully, looking to me for support.

I groaned again. "I suppose we could clear the worst of the droppings up," I said. "But when we've done that, *we're off.*"

"Count me out. I'm off now," said Baxter. He looked to Sam, who always does exactly what Baxter tells him, but not today. Sam was on the side of the animals.

"I think we should finish separating them out," he said. "Then there won't be any more babies."

"Look, it won't take long," I promised Baxter. "After that we'll have to tell someone." I was thinking of my mum. She'd know what to do.

"Do we have to?" Dingdong said, arranging

toast and tea on a tray with a little place mat. She looked like she'd move in and play housekeeper given half the chance.

"Yes, we do!" I insisted.

Dingdong shrugged and went back upstairs.

After he'd eaten three rounds of toast, Baxter said, "Right, come on then, let's get this job done. You find a tea towel," he told me. "I'll wash up."

He rolled up his sleeves and got stuck in. In no time, we were all paddling in soapy water, but I didn't complain. At least he was doing his share for once.

Next, I emptied my pockets of all the loose gerbils and Sam sorted the males and females into separate containers.

There was no sawdust so I grabbed a few newspapers off the hall floor and left the gerbils to make their own bedding.

Then I found a brush and swept up all the stinky stuff.

Half an hour later, despite all our hard work, the place still looked a sorry mess. And Dingdong hadn't yet come back down.

"This is a mug's game," Baxter complained, throwing in the dishcloth. I agreed. The biggest problem was the animals needed food and we could only find empty sacks. The runaway gerbils had clearly got there before us.

"I think I should go and get my mum," I said.

"Well, you'd better do it quick," Baxter told me, "before Mary Poppins comes downstairs, because she's not going to be happy."

So I left Sam still sorting the gerbils, and Baxter making himself *another* round of toast.

I wasn't looking forward to trying to explain any of this to my mum. By the time I reached home I still hadn't got a decent story sorted, but it hardly mattered. The minute she saw me she went up like a rocket. So I just stood there and waited until the fireworks were over.

CHAPTER SEVEN

"**W**here have you been?" she shrieked. "You've been gone hours. Carol's out of her mind worrying about Sam. We were about to call the police! Where are the others? What have you all been doing?"

Does your mum do that: keep on firing questions at you, giving you no chance to answer? When she finally drew breath, I'd forgotten what she'd asked.

"Can I have a sandwich?" I said. "I'm starving."

"No, you can not," she told me. "Not before I get some answers."

I sighed. I knew it'd be a tactical error to start with why we'd gone to the old lady's house in the first place. So I skipped that bit. I went straight to the old lady's broken ankle. It paid off. Mum calmed down then and agreed to come round.

"I'll just have to get changed first," she said. "And ring Carol."

"I should get back, Mum," I said. "The others are waiting for me."

She tutted but then nodded. "I'll follow you."

"Mu-u-um," I said before I left, and I knew I was pushing my luck by now, "would you mind ringing the R.S.P.C.A for us?"

Mum shook her head. "Which poor animals have you been mistreating now, Robin?" she asked, in a disappointed voice.

"Not *us*," I said. "We found them already running wild, with nothing to eat."

"*Which* animals?" she repeated.

When I told her they were gerbils she sighed, as if that was a bit better than she'd feared.

"I don't think the R.S.P.C.A will want to know about a couple of gerbils."

"No, Mum," I said, "but they might want to know about a couple of hundred."

"*A couple of hundred!*" she almost screamed.

"That's just a guestimate," I told her. "It might be a lot more. They won't stay still long enough for us to count them."

"Oh, Robin," she said, wearily, "what have you got yourself into this time?"

When I got back Baxter was sitting with his feet on the kitchen table *still* eating toast. Sam was again trying to coax a pair of gerbils into getting it together. He wasn't having any luck with these two either.

"I don't know what I'm doing wrong," he complained.

Baxter and me rolled our eyes. I suggested if he left them to get on with it on their own, *without an audience*, they might be more willing.

I suddenly heard a loud thudding sound coming from the old lady's bedroom.

"Sounds like she's fallen out of bed," I said.

But Baxter shook his head, "That's been going on for the last ten minutes. Maybe you'd better go and look."

I popped my head nervously round the bedroom door and found Dingdong leaping around like the Sugar Plum Fairy.

"What do *you* want?" she asked, rather rudely in my opinion.

"We thought there must be an elephant up here...*skipping*," I said, grinning. Dingdong wasn't amused. "Anyway, we're leaving soon," I told her.

"Oh, what a pity," said the old lady, "I was really enjoying the dancing."

"I'll be down in a minute," Dingdong said, dismissing me.

I couldn't wait to get downstairs and tell the other two what she'd been up to. But I suddenly stopped in my tracks.

"By the way," Dingdong called after me, "I hope you've still got Leonardo safe. I don't want him getting mixed up with all those wild gerbils down there."

My feet *froze* on the spot; my hands flew automatically to my pockets. But I knew it was too late. I'd emptied them – *both pockets* – into any one of the many containers in the kitchen. I hadn't the least idea which one Leonardo was in.

My mum's words echoed in my ears: *Oh, Robin, what have you got yourself into this time?*

By the time I raced into the kitchen, I'd forgotten why I'd gone upstairs in the first place.

"*Well*?" Baxter asked, gesturing for information.

"Oh, that," I said, "Dingdong dancing."

"So why do *you* look as if you've just laid an egg?"

"*I've lost Leonardo,*" I told him.

"You can't have lost him. He must be here somewhere." But then the truth dawned on him, too. "Oh. *Woah*! You are *dead*, man."

"*Dead*," echoed Sam.

"Come on, you two," I said. "You've got to help me find him."

"I dunno if I can," Baxter grinned. He looked like he was going to enjoy watching me disappear under a dollop of *doodoo*. "I mean, one gerbil looks just like another to me."

"At least we've got them sorted by sex now," I said. "So that's half the battle."

But as I grabbed the closest of the male cages another problem hit me. I'd never paid the least attention to Leonardo. I couldn't have said exactly *what* he looked like.

"Was he more brown or more grey, would you say?" I asked, desperately.

"Search me," Baxter shrugged.

"Come on, Sam," I pleaded. "You can recognize him, surely."

66

Sam lifted out each gerbil in the cage and studied it before putting it back. "No. No. N-n-o. Definitely not. Could be…" he said, handing it to me.

"*Could be?*" I repeated. Sam shrugged.

I started off a new container of *possible Leonardos*.

We'd only got through a few cages when there was a knock at the front door. I raced to get there, praying it was my mum, and not the R.S.P.C.A.

"Oh, *Robin*," she said again, as she came hurrying in. With just a glance she seemed to take in the state of the place, which luckily took her attention off me.

"Where is the old lady?" she asked.

I pointed upstairs. "Second door on the right. Dingdong's with her."

"What's her name?"

"Mrs Gum…" I stopped myself just in time. "I don't know," I shrugged.

This only made my mum shake her head again.

"Dingdong probably knows," I added, lamely.

I dashed back to carry on the search. I sent up a prayer that neither the R.S.P.C.A., nor Dingdong, would appear in the kitchen for at least the next ten minutes. With more than twenty-five cages still to go through, it felt about as hopeless as trying to find a needle in a haystack!

CHAPTER EIGHT

OK, time for another of my top secrets for
success.

*Every business needs an efficient operating
system* – and that's what I needed now. It would
have to be *fast* and efficient if I was going to get all
those cages checked in the next ten minutes.

I stopped for a moment to think it through,
then got to work.

I sat Sam at the kitchen table, then I lined up
the first few cages in front of him. As he finished
checking each cage, I slid the next one along, like

it was on a conveyor belt. It was brilliant. Sam didn't have to move from the spot. I ran round him neatly stacking the sorted ones out of the way.

It was working like a dream – until Baxter decided to help. I suddenly turned and saw him adding cages from the female pile to the end of the queue. "Woah! Woah! Woah!" I almost screamed. "Not those."

"Keep your rug on," he said, looking rather hurt. "I was only trying to help."

"It's just that I've got an operating system," I said.

"Oh, is that what you call it?" he said, sulkily, retreating to the breakfast bar for more slices of toast.

As it turned out, the system was far from foolproof, anyway. Every now and again Sam handed me an odd female that he'd somehow missed the first time round.

But we were finally left with a cage of six *possible Leonardos*. To be honest, they looked like identical sextuplets to me.

"So, which one is it?" I asked Sam.

He shrugged. "I'm not sure. Could be any of them."

I stared at the cage willing the real Leonardo to pop up its paw and say, "OK, game's over. It's me. I'm the one." But that was never going to happen.

I ♥ GERBILS

"Just choose one, for goodness sake," Baxter said, bored with the whole business.

"Choose? How can I choose?"

"Look, if we can't tell one from the other, what makes you think Dingdong's going to be able to?"

Baxter had a point, and anyway I'd finally run out of time. There was another knock at the door. This time it had to be the R.S.P.C.A.

I closed my eyes, reached into the cage and picked one at random. I didn't even bother to look at it. What was the point? I put it carefully in my pocket and went to let them in.

There were two very big men in yellow jackets standing there, looking scarily like policemen.

"Is your mum in, son?" they asked. They clearly thought no one of my age could possibly be trusted to hold a sensible conversation.

"She's upstairs," I said, "but the animals…" I spread my arms to indicate the whole house, "are *everywhere.*"

"So I see," said the taller one, looking straight

72

over my head into the hall. He said his name was Joe.

"Phew, there's a bit of a whiff," said the other one, who was called Dave. He gave me an accusing look. "When did you last clean these out?"

"They're not mine," I said. "We found them like this."

By now Baxter and Sam were behind me. The men came into the hall and began to see the size of the problem.

"Good heavens! How many are there?" Joe asked.

"We've lost count," said Baxter. "But if you think this is a lot, wait till you see the kitchen."

"And the bathroom," I added.

The two men rolled their eyes and followed us along the hall. Working for the R.S.P.C.A. you might think these two would have seen everything. But I don't think they'd seen anything like this. They kept gasping and asking us questions we couldn't really answer.

After all our work, I was a bit insulted with the way they went on about the mess the place was in.

"What a disgusting state," said Dave.

"Shocking," agreed Joe.

I almost said, "You should have seen it before." But looking round the kitchen, thick with toast crumbs and jam and screwed up newspaper and dirty wet footprints, I wasn't sure we had improved things very much.

At least, I thought, we'd saved them some time by sexing the animals. But they seemed doubtful we'd even got that right.

"Not easy to sex, gerbils, are they, Joe?" Dave said, shaking his head.

"Not before five weeks," Joe agreed. "And I'd say a lot of these are younger than that, wouldn't you, Dave?"

"Definitely," Dave nodded.

I anxiously put my hand in my pocket and gently squeezed the gerbil I hoped and prayed was Leonardo.

"Now, if you'll just show us where we can find the old lady," said Dave. "Then maybe you lads can help us get them all loaded into the van."

"Are you taking them *all* away?" Baxter asked.

"Let's see what the old lady has to say."

Just then Dingdong reappeared. It seemed the only thing on the old lady's mind was more cups of tea.

"We'll go on up then," said Joe.

Dingdong watched them suspiciously, "Who are they?" she asked.

Baxter, the coward, looked away – and so did Sam. I could think of a few good stories, but I knew in the end she was still going to go ballistic. So I decided to just get it over with.

"They're from the R.S.P.C.A.," I said, "and, before you explode, it was a joint decision."

Dingdong didn't explode. Quite the opposite, she looked at us like we'd stabbed her *and* the old lady in the back. "I just hope you're all proud of yourselves," she told us. "Especially *you*," she pointed at me.

Then she took the tray back upstairs, a cloud of disappointment trailing after her. I couldn't see why I'd been singled out.

But Baxter grinned. "Not such a blue-eyed boy any more," he said, winking at me.

CHAPTER NINE

Soon after that, there was a stream of people coming and going: a lady from social services, a nurse, a doctor, and finally an ambulance crew arrived. Mum told us we could leave the front door open and stay out of the way in the kitchen, which suited us just fine.

But not Dingdong. She was up and down stairs making tea like she was running a café. I wouldn't have cared but she treated us like we were her kitchen slaves.

I wondered, not for the first time, why

girls are so…*different*?

It's like Baxter always says, they just *are*. It's one of the basic laws of the universe, he reckons, like gravity or black holes.

"Anyway," Baxter said, lowering his voice, "I think we should pocket a couple of gerbils each now, while we've got the chance. Let's face it: no one's ever going to know. And if we don't, the whole bloomin' day's been a complete and utter waste of time."

I had to admit he was right. We'd been here nearly all day, for goodness sake. And they were just going to be taken away, in any case.

"As long as we leave the money on the table," I agreed.

I knew that in a pet shop four pounds fifty-five wouldn't pay for half a gerbil, never mind half a dozen. But it meant I could just about square it with myself.

We quickly chose what we hoped was a male and female each. I put my pair in my left pocket – well away from Leonardo – so there'd be no more mix-ups.

We'd only just done it when Mum came hurrying into the kitchen.

"Have you seen Mrs Haddock's handbag?" she asked. "They're taking her to the hospital and she's panicking about it."

Mrs Haddock! Baxter and me couldn't keep our faces straight. We just couldn't. Yeah, yeah, I know, it's only someone's name. But imagine if it was yours. Imagine the grief you'd get at school if you were called Harry or Hattie Haddock.

I managed to stop grinning and pass Mum the black bag that I'd seen on top of the microwave. She checked inside for a purse, which was what the old lady had been worrying about.

"I hope you haven't touched this?" Mum said, giving me a meaningful look.

I knew what she meant and it made me pretty mad, until I remembered the two gerbils in my pocket that didn't strictly belong to me. Then she noticed the four pounds fifty-five on the table. "Whose is this?"

I didn't dare look at Baxter. "Must be Mrs Haddock's," I said. "It was there when we got here."

Mum put it away in the purse. "I wish old people wouldn't leave money lying around," she said. "Just asking for trouble. Now I'm going to the hospital with her and I want you all to go straight home and get something to eat. Do not *under any circumstances*," she emphasised, "go anywhere else until I'm back. Is that clear?"

"We're just going to help the men load the gerbils into the van first," I told her. "Then we will."

She nodded. "But *when I get home* I shall want a full account – with *all* the details. Understood?"

I nodded back. I'd have to make sure my story was watertight before then. My mum's interrogations are awesome; she could teach the C.I.D. a few tricks.

Before she left, I asked Mum how long Mrs Haddock had been up there. I kept thinking about what Dingdong and Baxter had said.

"Only a couple of days," she told us. "But she's clearly not been coping for much longer than that. So it's a good job you found her. You did the right thing – *this time*."

After the ambulance left, we carried out the cages to the van and helped Dave and Joe stack them four high and six deep.

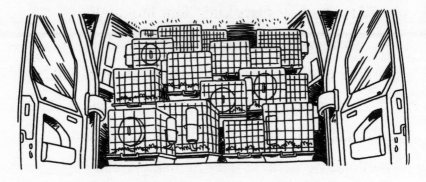

Before they left they did a final tour of the house. "I think that's the last of them," Dave said, "unless, of course, you lads have got any hidden up your trouser legs."

They laughed, as if it was so funny. We weren't laughing, not because it was a bad joke, but because it was too close to the truth.

Before they drove off, Dingdong asked them how many gerbils they thought there were altogether.

Dave and Joe frowned, while they did the sums. They'd counted sixty-two containers, they said, and a few of those had as many as a dozen in them.

"At a guess…" Dave said, "four hundred?"

"Perhaps more," said Joe.

Four hundred! We could hardly believe it, but it turned out to be even more than that.

A few days later they let us know the total count had been…*five hundred and fifty-one*! *Unbelievable!*

With all the cages gone the place looked an even worse mess.

"Don't worry," the lady from social services told us. "We'll make sure it's cleaned before Mrs Haddock comes home."

"She's definitely coming home, though?" Dingdong asked.

"Oh, yes," the lady said. "But not for a few

weeks, not until she's properly better. You've done her a real favour," she told us, but somehow it didn't feel like that.

She locked the door and waved goodbye as she headed for her car. When I looked back at the house, it felt as if we'd been there for days, not just a few hours.

"Come on," said Baxter. "My stomach thinks my mouth's on strike."

"That'd be a day to look forward to," Dingdong said and we all laughed. It was a pretty unlikely event.

Then Dingdong held her hand out to me. "Hand him over," she said.

I tried to act naturally, but I could feel my heart thump against my ribs. I reached into my right pocket and took out the single gerbil. I passed it over and held my breath, sending up a silent prayer: *Let it be him! Please, let it be him!*

Dingdong gave the gerbil a quick peck on the nose. "Who's my gorgeous boy?" she said, tucking him inside her trackie top.

Phew! Oh, thank you, I breathed. Thank you. I'd escaped, for now, at least.

CHAPTER TEN

O ver the next few weeks our gerbil business really started to take shape. We had three breeding pairs and it was soon obvious that all the females were pregnant.

Sam was in gerbil heaven, looking after them all, cleaning them out…leaving Baxter and me free to work on our business plan. This basically meant me doing lots of sums, and Baxter doing lots of whittling. He said, hadn't I ever heard of *delegation?* It looked far more like skiving to me.

Our biggest problem, though, was cash-flow. The problem was we didn't have any. We had to use all our pocket money to buy feed for the gerbils. But as I tried to remind everyone, for the first time in ages we had the prospect of making some *real* money.

So things were looking pretty good. Then one morning Dingdong came into the shed carrying Leonardo, asking Sam to have a look at him. Alarm bells started ringing.

"Why?" I asked quickly, but tried to look as if I couldn't care less. "What's wrong with him?"

"He's…different somehow," she said. "He won't go near his wheel and he used to be such a little demon on it."

Sam looked at me but I looked down, frightened I might give myself away. I kept scribbling random numbers on a piece of paper.

Sam pretended to inspect the gerbil but quickly handed it back. "Look's OK to me," he muttered.

"He's fatter, though, don't you think?"
Dingdong persisted.

"*Fatter*?" I suddenly found myself squeaking.

"Yeah, much fatter. I mean, if he wasn't a
male," she laughed, "I'd be thinking...you know..."
she rolled her eyes towards the cages with the
pregnant females in.

I just kept thinking, Oh, no, surely that's not
possible.

But, of course, it was.

And so, as the other three females got closer to having babies, so did Leonardo! In the end there was no doubting it.

I don't know how we managed it, but we somehow persuaded Dingdong she'd always been wrong about Leonardo. That *he* had always been a *she*. She'd just never realised.

"No need to be embarrassed," Baxter told her, generously. "Dave and Joe told us it's really difficult to sex gerbils."

"Even *they* get it wrong sometimes," I agreed, slightly bending the truth.

To our amazement she swallowed it. She didn't seem to take it too badly either. Probably, the fact that her gerbil was having babies made up for any other disappointment. And overnight Leonardo de Caprio turned into Angelina Jolie.

So, anyway, I'd got away with that one,

which was an excellent result. Unfortunately,
The Genuine Gerbil Factory wasn't another.

After five weeks we had our first litters: three lots
of five babies. We kept back three pairs to carry on
breeding with. But we now had quite a few to sell
to the local pet shop.

"We're going to be so rich," Baxter announced,
rubbing his hands.

I was pretty excited too. I was looking forward
to driving a hard bargain with the pet shop owner.
I'd got it all worked out in my head. So it was a bit
of a blow when the old guy refused to haggle. He
turned us away, saying, "Not buying any gerbils
right now, thanks."

The same thing happened at the second shop.

And then again at the third and last shop we
tried. It was there we discovered the reason that
no one was buying gerbils at the moment.

"Sorry, lads," the pet shop owner told us, "the bottom's fallen out of the gerbil market. The local R.S.P.C.A. are giving away *hundreds*. So why would anyone want to buy one?"

We were absolutely gutted, but Baxter, as usual, did the most complaining: "When I think about the bloomin' waste of time. Not to mention the money! All my pocket money's gone on feeding those wretched rodents," he grumbled.

"All *our* pocket money," I reminded him.

And now we'd got twenty gerbils we'd have to keep on feeding – unless we could find a way to offload them.

Fortunately, with my marketing skills, I did manage it. By the end of the week I'd persuaded the kids at school to take them all. We had to throw in the cages for free – and the rest of the feed. But sometimes you just have to cut your losses.

At least after that my pocket money was my own again. Or it was, until I got fleeced by Dingdong. I should have seen that coming.

One night, a week later, Dingdong knocked on our door and told my mum, "Mrs Haddock's coming home. I'm going to buy a bunch of flowers to welcome her."

"That's a very nice idea, Annabelle," Mum

said. "Isn't it, Robin?"

I shrugged like I had no opinion on the matter, which, to be honest, I hadn't.

"I thought you might like to put something towards it," Dingdong said, looking *me* straight in the eye.

The thing is she'd already suggested it earlier on, when we were in the shed. And we'd all said no way, José. But in front of my mum she knew I was a pushover.

I stood there squirming while Mum gave me a hug. "I'm so proud of you, Robin," she said. "You're so thoughtful."

If looks could kill, Dingdong would have been hung, drawn and quartered on the spot. But what did she care – she'd got my money.

Obviously, I didn't tell Baxter about this. So just keep it to yourself, will you?

I still say we could have struck gold. We just got into the gerbil business at the worst possible time, but we weren't to know that.

So my final business tip for today: *when one door closes, another door opens.*

And sure enough it did.

Our next scheme didn't only have legs, it had a full head of hair! No kidding. It was set to be a *hair-raising success.*

But, enough of the jokes.

Next time I see you I'll tell you all about it.

The Happy
Hair Saloon

Rose Impey

CHAPTER ONE

Hi there. I thought you'd be back – for a few more of my hot business tips. And the next instalment of the *Get Rich Quick Club's* stunning story of success.

OK, but the shed's smelling even more rank than ever today, so let's sit out here – in our office extension. Grab a couple of Jammy Dodgers first – better still, bring the packet.

The seats are from Baxter's dad's old van. We rescued them when it finally died and went to the tip. Pretty neat, huh?

We often sit out here, tossing around ideas. At least, I do; Baxter just *whittles*. He says whittling gives him inspiration, but there hasn't been much evidence of that.

Luckily, I've noticed that when the brain cells aren't working and you most need a hand, fate often helps out.

Like a few weeks ago when Dingdong came round, giving us her big *hairy* tale of woe, and *just like that* a new business venture was launched. Well, not exactly just like that. But it didn't take me long to see the possibilities.

And it really was all thanks to Dingdong.

I know we're always moaning about her. But, the truth is, things could be much worse. We could be living next door to Nigella Horseface.

No, that's not her real name – it's
Horseforth – but Horseface suits
her better. She's a friend of
Dingdong's and, compared
to her, Dingdong's an absolute
diamond. You'll see when you
meet her. And, I promise
you, you *will* meet her!

But back to the story. This time we really
did make a packet. Yes! Real money. In fact,
it was the easiest money we'd ever made.

So, listen and learn, my friend. Listen
and learn.

It was a Friday afternoon. We'd finished school
early because it was half term. We were sitting
out here with our catapults, taking potshots at
this old stuffed donkey Baxter had painted a bull's
eye on. I was slaughtering Baxter, mainly because

he wasn't giving the game his full attention.

"Beat that if you can," I challenged him.

Baxter hardly lifted his nose out of his book. It was on tying knots. Have I already mentioned how obsessed Baxter gets? He's like a dog with a bone.

"So, what're we up to this week?" I asked, hoping someone else might come up with an idea for once.

We'd got the whole of half term stretching before us with plenty of opportunity for money-making. But Baxter clearly had no plans, apart from tying up anything that stood still for two minutes.

Apparently, he'd been practicing on Sam all week and Sam had the rope burns to prove it. I don't envy him having to share a bedroom with Baxter. No way, José.

Sam was busy too, trying to train Rooney,

his pet rat. He'd made this maze in a cardboard box. At the end of each run he'd put different flavoured crisps. He wanted to see which flavour the rat would keep going back to. Can you believe *chilli and chocolate* was Rooney's favourite so far? Baxter and me agreed we would *never* eat chilli and chocolate.

"Unless we were lost in the jungle with no hope of rescue," I said.

"And only then after we'd eaten each other," Baxter added.

So Sam was no help either. And, for once, my own head was as empty as the cash box.

But then it came straight out of left field.

"*Err err! Err err!*" Baxter muttered under his breath. "Dingdong alert."

As soon as we saw her we could tell she'd been blubbing. At first, no one asked what was wrong, although to be honest I was curious. Baxter was never going to ask, but the longer she stood there the harder I was finding it to keep my mouth shut. In the end I said. "What's up with you?"

Baxter fluttered his eyelashes, to let me know he thinks I'm a bit of a girl sometimes.

"I'm going to the hairdresser's," she wailed.

"Big hairy deal," I said. Sorry, no pun intended.

"Yeah, it's not like going to the dentist," Baxter said, dismissively.

"No," she cried. "It's much, much worse. My Granny Mac's here. And you know what happened last time!"

Suddenly it all came clear.

Obviously, being their cousin, Dingdong shares one grandma with the Baxters. But she's also got a Scottish one, Granny Mackenzie, who's *seriously* scary. Baxter wouldn't mess with her; even Baxter's dogs wouldn't mess with Granny Mac.

Last time Dingdong went to visit her, Granny Mac dragged her off to this old ladies' hairdresser. Apparently, Dingdong cried – *all the way home from Scotland.*

To be fair, they had almost scalped her. At school she wore a hat for six weeks, but everyone still called her *Pudding Head.*

"At least you're not going to *her* hairdresser this time," I said, cheerfully.

"No, but she's already phoned and told them to

cut it all off! It's not fair!" she wailed again.

She was rubbing her eyes with what I *thought* was a screwed up handkerchief – until I looked closer.

"Is that, by any chance, a ten pound note?" I asked. "It seems an awful lot of money…for a hair cut," I said.

I glanced at Baxter and he glanced back. Sometimes I think we're telepathic. He knew *exactly* what I was thinking.

"'Specially if you only want a *bit* off…" Baxter agreed.

"More a trim than a cut, then," I said.

"How hard can that be?" he shrugged.

"Hardly rocket science," I said.

Dingdong stopped blubbing. Her eyes were flicking between us like she was watching a tennis match. Finally she said to me, "Are you saying *you'd* do it?"

"Or Baxter. Or both of us," I added quickly when her face dropped. "For a fair price, of course."

"Sam! Go get the scissors," Baxter ordered.

Sam muttered and grumbled but, as usual, did as he was told.

"OK," I said, getting up and opening the door to the shed. "If you'd just like to step inside our *salon*."

I stood back while Baxter led Dingdong firmly by the arm into the shed. "Now, what exactly did *madam* have in mind?" he asked, grinning at me over his shoulder.

CHAPTER TWO

Before she could change her mind, we'd backed
Dingdong into the swivel chair. Baxter went a
bit wild spinning it round to adjust the height.

"Stop making me dizzy!" she complained.

Next he wrapped an old sheet round her neck.

"Yuk! That stinks!" she complained again.

To be fair, it *was* the one Sam uses when

he cleans out his gerbils.

"Perhaps madam would like a cup of coffee?" I suggested.

"Good idea," Baxter agreed, nodding towards the kettle. Clearly I was the one expected to make it.

Dingdong was back to her old bossy self as well, now she'd stopped crying. "You'd better hurry up," she said, looking at her watch. "There'll be trouble if I'm not home in an hour."

"What do you want me to do?" Baxter asked. "Chew it off?"

"We're just waiting for the scissors," I reminded her.

"So, who's going to do it?" she asked.

"I am," said Baxter.

"He is," I agreed. I'm not stupid. If things went wig-shaped I didn't want to be the one holding the scissors.

Dingdong didn't look too happy about that. For some reason, she seemed to have more confidence in me than in Baxter.

"Relax," Baxter told her. "It'll be like a joint effort."

"Yeah, yeah, I'll be advising," I reassured her.

"Well, I only want a couple of centimetres off the back," she said. "I don't want anything off the fringe. Make sure it's dead straight. And if you cut my ear off you're dead, both of you. Understood?"

"Ohhh, if you're going to be this difficult a customer…" Baxter said, dragging the sheet off her and tipping Dingdong unceremoniously out of the chair.

"Makes no odds to us," I agreed. "We were trying to do you a favour."

Baxter muttered under his breath, "*Pudding Head.*"

Dingdong collapsed back into the chair,

like a deflated balloon. "It's just a bit scary," she admitted. "Swear you'll do it properly and you won't mess about."

"On my Ray Mears DVD collection," Baxter promised.

"*On your Swiss Army Knife!*" she raised him.

"OK, whatever," he agreed. "Let's just get on with it."

Sam had finally returned with the scissors, fortunately hidden behind his back. He handed them quietly to Baxter who waved them over Dingdong's head at me as if to say, "What the *heck* am I supposed to do with these?"

Sam had brought his mum's *pinking shears*. You know…the sort with zigzag edges. I shrugged, Baxter shook his head, then began by grabbing a handful of hair.

"Owww!" Dingdong complained. "Not so rough!"

She looked more like someone about to have a whole set of teeth out than a haircut. Although, to be honest, I'd have been nervous in her place. Baxter may be my best mate, but he's the last person I'd want let loose with a pair of scissors that close to my face.

But, sometimes, even Baxter is full of surprises…

I bet you thought he'd go at it like a madman let loose with an axe. So did I. But he didn't.

Instead, he nibbled away a little bit at a time. For the next quarter of an hour Baxter snip-snipped his way round one side, then snip-snipped round the other. To be honest, considering he was using pinking shears, it wasn't *bad*.

On the other hand…it wasn't great. Even though he did his best to make sure it was straight, it sort of dipped up and down like the edge of a lace curtain.

As if she had eyes in the back of her head, Dingdong suddenly said, "It'd better be the same length all over – or else."

"Give me a chance," Baxter snapped.

"I think it needs a bit more off here," I pointed out. "And here…and here…and here…"

Unfortunately, every time Baxter corrected one problem – it just created another.

"You know what this reminds me of?" he said, as he snipped. "That time our Wayne made a table in woodwork class. He kept shortening one leg after another to get it level. When he brought it home he tried to pretend it was always meant to be a footstool."

"I am here, you know," Dingdong reminded him, "and I'm not a table or a footstool. Are you nearly done?"

To be honest we were all getting bored by now. We stood back and looked at Dingdong's head from every angle. The problem was: from every angle it looked different. But Baxter didn't know what else to do with it, so he said, "Yeah, you're done," and he pulled the sheet off her.

"So, show me what it looks like," Dingdong said. "Like they do in a proper hairdressers, you know, back and front. With a mirror!"

"Sam! Go get a mirror," Baxter ordered.

Sam groaned and went off again – taking nearly as long as he had over the scissors.

Baxter and me stood around waiting like spare parts, while Dingdong nervously tugged at her hair. She seemed relieved that it still covered her ears at least. Things couldn't be too bad. What she couldn't tell by touch alone was that the bottom went up and down like a fairground ride. And, for some reason, it was sticking out now, like it had a whole life of its own.

I just knew she was going to throw a mega wobbly when she saw it. Any minute now we'd all have to run for cover.

Sam came back staggering under the weight of his mum's mirror. It was the big one from their sitting room wall.

"You'd better not drop that," Baxter told him, "or you'll have seventy years bad luck."

"It's actually *seven* years," I corrected him.

"Oh, no," Baxter corrected me. "If he breaks

mum's mirror he'll be in deep *doodoo* the rest of
his sorry little life."

As I helped Sam lift the mirror so that
Dingdong would be able to see her new
improved haircut, Baxter told her, "Close
your eyes first. I'll tell you when to open them."

I thought, this is the point we should probably
leg it. But instead, we looked at one another, lifted
the mirror, then each held our breath…

"*Now…*" said Baxter. "Now you can look."

CHAPTER THREE

You know what it's like when you're waiting for a firework to go off – and it doesn't? Just waiting for the *bang*! Well, that's what it was like watching Dingdong.

She looked at herself, from every angle. She fluffed her hair about and did funny things with her mouth.

Finally, *finally*, she said, "Mmmm, I like it. It's…wild. Funky. It's…*different*."

It was different, all right. I'd never seen anything like it.

"If you say so," Baxter said, looking at me and grinning.

"That'll be ten pounds," I said, holding out my hand.

"Ten pounds? In your dreams," Dingdong said. "That's what a professional hairdresser would have cost. And you lot are far from professional. For a start, that sheet stank, the coffee was cold and there was no biscuit."

That was true, for once we'd run out of Jammy Dodgers.

"Maybe so," said Baxter, "but you got what you wanted. And you just said you liked it."

"So now you can pay up," I added, trying to sound menacing.

Dingdong rolled her eyes then, grudgingly, handed over the screwed up, tear-stained ten pound note. Then she went off home.

We were so excited we were almost dancing.

"Ten pounds!" I yelled. "Can you believe it?"

"Like taking biscuits off a baby," Baxter grinned.

He was right. It had to be the easiest money we'd ever made. That was when I realised our next business venture was staring us in the face.

"That's it!" I said. "We'll open up for business. You can do the haircuts, I'll be the manager. Just think how many kids at school hate going to the barber." I tried to keep the excitement out of my voice.

Baxter nodded. "They always take too much off," he agreed.

I glanced round the shed. "We'd have to clean up a bit. And get rid of some of these animals." Baxter and Sam looked like I'd just insulted them and their whole family. "And we'd need proper scissors."

"We can get scissors," Baxter shrugged.

"We might have to lower our prices," I suggested. Not everyone would be as desperate as Dingdong. "But as long as we undercut the local hairdressers we can't lose. We'll do a roaring trade over half term."

Start small; think big is another of my business mottoes. I could see it all now. We'd start with one salon, gradually open up a whole string of them all over Manchester, London, and finally, who knows…world domination!

But first we needed a business plan.

I grabbed a piece of paper and wrote:

1. Choose a business name – something snappy.
2. Check out the competition.
3. Think up an advertising campaign.

"OK. First let's choose a name," I said.

Baxter sat back and looked thoughtful. Thinking

up a good name's always one of our favourite bits.

"What about Baxter's Mega-Cool Cuts?" he suggested, modest as ever.

"Not bad," I said. "What about…Cheap Chops? That's short *and* snappy."

"Sounds like a butcher!" said Baxter. "What about Crop Shop? That's *snappy*."

"Yeah, but it sounds like they're going to get scalped."

"I know! I know!" he said, dramatically, drawing a finger across his throat. "Cut and *Dye*!"

He suddenly looked like Sweeny Todd, the demon barber, you know, the one who chopped people up and put them in pies.

"Too *scary*," I said. "We want to keep everyone happy..."

"While we take their money," Baxter grinned.

And that's when it came to me: *The Happy Hair Salon*.

Tell me, am I a genius, or *am I a genius*? Of course, if I *was* a genius, I wouldn't have left Baxter to make the sign, would I?

The next morning I couldn't believe my eyes.

"It's *salon*, Dummy," I said, "not *saloon*."

"I told him that," Sam chipped in.

"You did not," Baxter argued. "Anyway, no one'll notice."

"Of course people'll notice," I argued.

"Well, tough, it's the only spare sheet we've got," said Baxter.

Sometimes, don't you just wish you'd done the job yourself?

But that's another thing I've learned: in business *you have to choose your battles*. OK, I'd lost this one; it was time to move on to Number 2: *Check out the competition.*

An hour later the three of us were standing outside the local hairdressers and sticking out like two and a half sore thumbs. I'd told Baxter and Sam this was an *undercover operation* and not to draw attention to themselves.

I don't know why I bothered. We might as well have had signs over our heads saying: *Everyone, look at us! Look at us!*

Baxter was in full camo gear as usual, with his

precious frayed rope round his waist, and wearing sunglasses. Sam had insisted on bringing Rooney! He's trying to train the rat to ride on his shoulder. One or two older people looked like they might have a heart attack on the spot.

The hairdressers was called *Good Hair Daze*, which made me feel a bit better about Baxter's spelling mistake.

On a brighter note I could see what a money-spinner this hair business was going to be. There were loads of people waiting for appointments.

Sam had his nose pressed against the glass, staring inside.

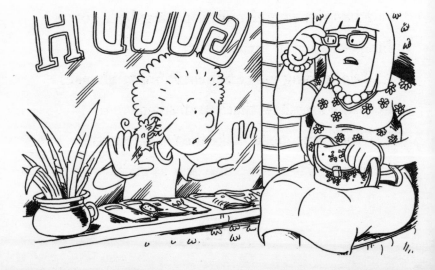

"Will you stop that," I hissed, but it was too late. A young girl came out and asked, pleasantly at first, if we were waiting for someone inside.

"No," said Baxter.

"Well, in that case," she said, changing her tone entirely, "can you clear off? You're making dirty marks on the window and Mister Julian doesn't like it."

"Mister Julian can lump it," said Baxter. "It's a free country."

I dragged Baxter and Sam across the road before we got into any more trouble. "We can see everything we need to from here," I said.

I'd brought a notebook and started a list of things to do.

"We're going to need a receptionist," I began.

"Dingdong'll do that," Baxter said.

"And someone to make the tea and do the brushing up."

"That'll be Sam," Baxter volunteered.

"No, it won't," Sam argued.

"Yes, it *will*," Baxter repeated, menacingly, "*because Sam's good at doing as he's told*."

"Like he has a choice," Sam muttered.

But there was one insurmountable problem, as far as Baxter could see. "Everyone's getting their hair washed," he said.

"Well, we won't be doing that," I said, firmly, in case it wasn't already blindingly obvious. Baxter didn't reply. "Because we've got no sink," I spelled it out. "*No running water?*"

"No," said Baxter, vacantly.

But you could see the cogs of what Baxter likes to call his brain starting to turn over.

That always makes me nervous. Like I said, when Baxter gets an idea into his head – he won't let it go.

CHAPTER FOUR

ord Sugar, you know, my all-time hero, says: *to be a business entrepreneur, you have to learn to delegate.* As far as I can see that just means giving other people the boring jobs, while you get on with the good stuff. But I wonder how Lord Sugar would manage if the only people he'd got to delegate to were Baxter and Sam. Honestly, every time I thought about that banner, I wanted to climb up there with a big felt pen.

At least when I got to the shed on Sunday morning things were looking up. All Sam's animal cages were outside on the path and Baxter had opened the shed windows and door to clear the air. For the first time you could walk in without coughing.

In the middle of the floor there was a blue baby bath.

"What's that for?" I asked, suspiciously. "And that?" A hosepipe poked through the window and hung down the wall.

"A *sink*," Baxter said, looking pretty pleased with himself. "And running water! Turn it on, Sam," he yelled.

The hose sprung into life and water sprayed out like a high power jet, flooding the whole shed in seconds. Baxter and me raced for the door already soaked to the skin, but we hit it at the same time and managed to get stuck in the doorway. Baxter fell backwards, dragging me with him, right into the line of fire. The hose carried on

throwing itself around the shed like a demented snake, giving us a second soaking.

"Sam!!! Too much!" Baxter bellowed as we raced again for the door. "Turn it off!"

When it was at last turned off, Sam complained, "You never said how far to turn it."

I stood there dripping and shivering but Baxter suddenly rushed back inside. He carried out a pile of sopping wet magazines. "Now look what you did," he accused Sam. "I *borrowed* these 'specially." He laid them carefully in the sun to dry out.

To be honest, I couldn't see kids from school wanting to read recipes and soppy love stories in Baxter's mum's magazines. But I didn't say anything. I left him to it and helped myself to a towel. There was a whole pile he'd obviously also *borrowed* from his mum.

Just then Dingdong turned up. It was the first time we'd seen her since Friday. I'd been wondering if her haircut had gone down badly at home. But she still looked happy with it.

"What did Granny Mac say?" I asked her.

"What do you think?" Dingdong rolled her eyes. "She said it was like flushing a ten pound note down the toilet. She's gone home now, thank goodness." She looked around at the chaos. "What's going on here?"

"We're opening a hairdressers," I said, pointing to the sign. I hoped she wouldn't notice the spelling mistake. If she did, she didn't mention it.

"You *are* joking," she said, as though we'd told her we were taking a trip to Mars.

"What do you mean?" Baxter asked, offended. "I seem to remember you were happy enough with your haircut."

"You can be the receptionist," I told her.

"Great big hairy deal," she said. "Anyway, who on earth would come here for a haircut?"

"Loads of people," I said. "Kids from school."

Dingdong looked up for any passing pigs flying by. But I was determined not to let her undermine our confidence.

"We should have a dummy run," I suggested.

"Good idea," said Baxter. "Get in the chair."

"Not me," I said, jumping like I'd just been stung.

"Been there, done that, got the haircut," Dingdong grinned.

That only left one person. "Aw, why me?" Sam

whined, as if the answer wasn't dead obvious.

"Hair wash first," Baxter said, reaching for the hose-pipe.

"No way," Sam said, backing off.

Sam's always hated getting his hair washed since he was a baby. He's terrified of shampoo in his eyes.

"Let's skip hair washing," I suggested. "Just cut it dry."

Baxter looked at me with a pitying expression. "D'you want this to be a professional outfit?" he asked, "Either we do this properly or we don't do it at all."

I gave a big sigh. Sometimes there's no arguing with Baxter.

"Go get your gear," he told Sam.

Sam came back minutes later wearing swimming trunks and *a pair of swimming goggles*. The Baxters really are the craziest family.

Sam knelt down over the baby bath and Baxter poured a great dollop of soap over his head.

Dingdong grabbed the bottle off him. "That's washing up liquid!" she squealed.

"It's all the same," Baxter told her, dismissively.

It clearly wasn't. Sam's head frothed up until it disappeared under a huge cloud of bubbles.

It took ages for Baxter to get rid of them all. In the process he almost flooded the shed *again*.

"From now on," I said, "any hair washing is going to be done *outside*."

Although it was a warm day, Sam was shivering, so Dingdong wrapped him in a couple of towels. Then Baxter started the serious business of cutting Sam's hair. I noticed he'd got a new pair of scissors. They were the sort my mum keeps in the kitchen to cut the rind off bacon. But they seemed to be doing the job OK.

Having done one haircut, Baxter was now acting like he'd been doing it all his life. He kept standing back and admiring his handiwork like a real poser.

When he'd finished, Dingdong said, "You'll need a hair dryer."

"Got one," Baxter said, smugly, reaching into a

box and producing one. No guesses whose it was. I dreaded the point Baxter's mum discovered all the things he'd *borrowed*.

Baxter gave me the hairdryer to plug in, like I was his assistant. I unplugged the kettle and switched it on. Within minutes Sam was yelling, "Oww! You're burning me!"

"I think you'd better let me do this," Dingdong said, taking over.

I had to admit, she looked like she knew what she was doing. She made Sam's hair stand up in little spikes.

"He looks like a girl," Baxter complained.

But Sam was happy. "It's cool!" he said. "Thanks, Dingdong."

Baxter went into a bit of a sulk. But I agreed with Sam, it did look pretty cool.

I thought we were probably as ready as we'd ever be.

"We'll open for business tomorrow," I announced.

"But who's going to come?" asked Dingdong. "Nobody even knows about it."

"Don't worry," I said, "they will. That's number 3 on the plan: *Advertising*. Meet you all back here straight after lunch."

CHAPTER FIVE

After lunch we all headed off to the park. On a Sunday there were always a few kids from school there, having a kick about.

I'd made a couple of posters, this time *without* spelling mistakes! Then I'd ingeniously joined them together to make a sandwich board. Pretty neat, if I say so myself.

"So, who wants to wear it?" I asked, hopefully.

"Do I look like I've lost my brain?" Baxter asked.

It was tempting, but I didn't reply.

Dingdong stared at me, daring me to suggest she wear it.

Even Sam said, "No way, Banksy."

To be fair it would have drowned him. So, in the end, I wore it myself. Sometimes, as a boss, you have to lead by example. And when you do, it's important to try to look cool, which isn't easy when everyone's screaming with laughter at you.

COOL CUTS AT HALF THE PRICE

HAPPY HAIR SALON

no more sad hair days

"Nice sandwich," the footballers shouted. "Pity about the filling."

"Great fashion – hope it spreads."

"Don't run off," they shouted, starting to aim at me. "We're feeling a bit peckish."

Yeah, it was pretty embarrassing. But you know what they say: there's no such thing as bad publicity. They're laughing now, I thought, but we'll have the last laugh – all the way to the bank.

Dingdong met a few of her friends and showed off her new haircut. When she came back, she said, "They're going to think about it. They've taken the number."

"What number?" I asked. I hadn't put one on the poster.

"Mine, of course," she said. "I am the receptionist, aren't I? And I think you'd better leave the shampooing to me as well. Baxter's far too heavy-handed."

"You already took over the hairdryer," Baxter complained.

"Yeah, yeah, we'll see," I said, briskly, trying to keep the peace. I could see those two coming to blows with hairbrushes any day soon.

"OK. I think we can leave it to word of mouth now," I said. "We don't want too many people turning up all at once, do we?"

"In your dreams," laughed Dingdong.

But she wasn't laughing the next morning.

Before we'd even opened up the shed, there was already a noisy queue forming. Oh, yes, I thought, so this is what success smells like.

I don't know who'd got there first, but everyone stood aside for Jake Johnson. He's the captain of the football team and top dude in our school. All the girls fancy him and all the boys want to be him. Not me, of course; probably not Baxter either, but everyone else.

"You'd better get this one right," I whispered to Baxter. "If Jake Johnson's happy the whole football team'll be beating down our door. Get it wrong and no one'll come. It's make or break."

"Oh, thanks," he said, his hand starting to shake. "No pressure then?"

Next Dingdong decided to have a complete meltdown at the thought of washing Jake Johnson's hair. You'd have thought I'd asked her to wash Leonardo de Caprio's. *The* Leonardo de Caprio – not Dingdong's gerbil.

"I can't do it," she kept telling me. "I just…
can't."

In the end the queue was getting even noisier.
It's times like that you just have to step up and be
the boss.

"Just do it," I told her. "Or I'll find someone
else who will."

So Dingdong took a deep breath and poured
shampoo on Jake's hair. This time it was proper
shampoo.

Luckily, with his eyes closed, Jake couldn't see
Dingdong had gone as pink as her T-shirt.

Then it was Baxter's turn. I have to admit,
he put on a good act, behaving like he was
hairdresser to the stars. You'd have thought Jake
Johnson was nothing compared to the celebs
Baxter was used to. He whistled while he worked.

By the time it came to the blow-drying,
Dingdong was a bit more relaxed. She managed

it OK, despite dropping the hairbrush a couple of times. Then we showed Jake the end result in the mirror and all kept our fingers tightly crossed.

Jake Johnson never has much to say. So we weren't disappointed when he only nodded and handed over the cash. "Five pounds, right?"

"That's right," I said, pocketing the money.

And we'd done it! We'd done our second paid hair cut and it hadn't been a disaster. Oh, boy, I thought, we are on a roll!

We got through the other boys, nearly all footballers, without any mishaps too. By then all the towels were wet, so it was a good job after that we had a quiet spell.

I noticed Sam sitting counting some money of his own. He'd been bringing people in the queue drinks of juice at 10p a cup.

"You usually get a *free* drink at the hairdresser's," Dingdong pointed out, "plus a little

Italian biscuit. You don't *usually* pay extra."

Sam shrugged. "No one complained," he said.

I secretly admired Sam, he's a real little wheeler-dealer in the making. And anyway, I thought, he's been doing his job. I'd seen him eagerly sweeping up the cut hair with a dustpan and brush.

But I suppose I should have guessed Sam would have his own reasons. Later I heard him bargaining with Dingdong.

"What do you mean 20p?" she complained. "I'm not paying 20p, even for a lock of Jake Johnson's hair." After a lot of argument, she finally knocked him down to 15p.

"I bet she's going to sleep with that under her pillow tonight," Baxter grinned at me. Honest! What are girls like?

But it had been a brilliant day so far. We'd already made twenty-one pounds! It would have been twenty-five, but a couple of the bigger kids like Matt Biggs had decided to haggle about the price. And, trust me, you don't haggle with Matt Biggs, not if you want to keep your looks.

Added to Dingdong's tenner we now had a grand total of thirty-one pounds – and it was still only Monday!

CHAPTER SIX

In case you're wondering: so what was the secret of our success? That's easy.

Like all the best businesses it was built on one simple but great idea. Take the toasted sandwich-maker. Toast's good; sandwiches are good; but *toasted sandwiches* – mmm, heaven in your hand! Someone must have seen that gap in the market and filled it. We were just doing the same.

Kids have to have haircuts; kids don't want haircuts. What do they want? To look like they haven't had one. It was that simple. It was a winning formula.

And it would have gone on winning as long as everyone stuck to the plan – *including Baxter*. But, like I've told you before, Baxter easily gets bored. He changes his mind more often than he changes his boxers.

That's why it's always important to have a good manager. My job was to keep him – and everyone else – on track. This also involved making sure they didn't murder each other!

"What time do you call this?" Baxter asked Dingdong the next morning, when she arrived ten minutes late. "Not very professional."

"Not that it's any of your business," she snapped, "but I had to help my mum."

"You need to get your priorities right," Baxter snapped back.

"*You* need to keep your beak out."

"*You* need to watch your lip."

"OK, OK," I said, trying to cool things. "It's not like we're overrun with customers."

It was disappointingly quiet compared with Monday. But before too long a girl from Year 5 turned up. Her name was Brenda Gull and she was dragging her little brother behind her. Sam recognised him from the reception class.

She looked round suspiciously at first, but finally said, "He doesn't want much off."

"We never take much off," I told her.

"And he doesn't like having his hair washed."

"We can cut it dry," I said, ignoring Baxter muttering in the background.

"He can borrow my goggles," Sam volunteered.

Finally the little boy had his hair cut dry – but wearing Sam's goggles, anyway, just for the fun of it.

"He's only little, be nice to him," I whispered to Baxter.

"I'm always nice," said Baxter.

Brenda Gull watched Baxter's every move, but she seemed satisfied with the end result. She paid up and then said, "OK, I'll have one, too," like she was ordering a pizza.

Baxter and me looked at each other doubtfully. Brenda Gull has the longest hair I've ever seen. She can almost sit on it.

"I want it *all* off," she said.

"We only do trims," I told her quickly.

"But I'm sick of it. It's my mum who likes it, not me."

Alarm bells started ringing. I imagined her mum coming round here screaming, insisting we stick it back on again.

"How about a bit off today," I suggested, "then tomorrow, if you still want more off, you can come back again – for free."

I thought it was a pretty good offer. She looked doubtful, but finally agreed. Baxter did one of his big sighs and then made a start. Although he only cut about three centimetres off, it seemed to take him *hours*. He just couldn't get it level. It beats me how hairdressers do it!

Afterwards, Baxter said he was exhausted. "If she comes back tomorrow, *you* can cut it for nothing if you like. But I'm not. It's no way to do business."

Later, three of Dingdong's friends from school turned up: Tina, Meena and Serina. Baxter and me call them *The Three-inas*. When they all asked for the same haircut as Dingdong, Baxter started moaning.

"What are you, sheep?" he asked, waving his arms. "Can't you think for yourselves?" The girls stared at him as if he was mad. "Take a risk, live dangerously, try something different, for goodness sake."

Serina waited until he'd finished banging on, then she said, "So, can you do it like hers, *or not*?"

"Whatever!" Baxter growled.

Once again he got out the pinking shears and did his thing. The three girls went off dead happy, looking like a set of Dingdong clones.

Afterwards, Dingdong had the nerve to say, "I think I should get extra. If it wasn't for me, none of them would have come."

Baxter looked fit to explode so I said, "Don't worry, everyone'll get their share."

"I'd like mine *now*," Dingdong persisted, "before you blow it, like you usually do."

I told her, "This money's as safe as…a safe!"

"With the door open, maybe," she muttered.

It really bugs me the way Dingdong *always* gets the last word.

No one else came for a haircut that day. So we spent the rest of the afternoon with our feet up. I counted the money – a few times, in fact, just for the fun of it. Baxter, instead of whittling, sat leafing through his mum's magazines – looking at hairstyles!

This seemed to be his new obsession.

"I think we should get into colour next," he said.

"*What?*" I was praying he was joking.

"No, seriously, it'd bring in loads more kids."

I could imagine Baxter let loose with hair dye and half the local kids turning green overnight. "Let's not get too ambitious," I told him.

"You know, I might take this up, when I leave school," he said, completely seriously, "this hairdressing lark."

"What about survival? I thought you were going to be an explorer," I reminded him.

"Oh, yeah, that as well," he said. "But that's like being a professional footballer – a bit risky. You need a back-up plan. Hairdressing could be it." He paused. "From now on I'm going to call myself… *Mister Luigi.*"

I stared at him and asked what was wrong

with Billy? It was his name, after all.

"No glamour," he said. "Unless it was *Meester Beeeely* – with a French accent. That might work."

I shook my head but I didn't say anything. Baxter might be a five-star poser at times, but I couldn't argue with facts. He was good at this *hairdressing lark*. In only two days we'd made over fifty pounds! We were on a roll; we were *unstoppable*!

But you've probably heard what happens when *an unstoppable force meets an immovable object*? Head-on collision is what happens. Smash, crash, motorway pile-up. And it was coming our way, any time soon.

CHAPTER SEVEN

I bet you've got friends your mum's always warning you about who are mad, bad or dangerous to know. Friends you can't seem to keep away from – friends like Baxter.

The thing is: life's never boring around Baxter. You never know what he's going to do next – that's the good news. The bad news is: you really *never* know what he's going to do next.

The Happy Hair Saloon was going so well. After three days we'd got eighty-five pounds in the cash box. We could have doubled that, tripled it –

no probs. If Baxter hadn't got carried away.

I suppose I should have seen the warning signs, but I didn't.

On Thursday morning, really early, Baxter was sticking up pictures of hairstyles all over the shed. He'd gelled his own hair and done something funny with the front. He looked like a unicorn, but I decided not to mention it. There was no sign of Sam; that really should have tipped me off.

But our first customer was already waiting, so we had to get started. Brenda Gull had come back for a bit more off.

"What did your mum say?" I asked her.

"She hasn't even noticed," she told me, triumphantly. "I thought if I have a little bit off every day..."

Baxter gave me the evil eye. OK, it probably wasn't my best business decision ever. Anyway, he didn't take nearly so much trouble. I was pretty sure her mum was going to notice this time!

We were soon really busy. Some more footballers turned up, then more girls from our class arrived.

"There's quite a queue," I told them. "You might have to wait."

"We haven't come for a haircut," they said. "We want to see Sam."

"What for?" Baxter asked, suspiciously.

The girls went a bit pink. Sherry Summers, said, "We heard he'd got some hair to sell."

"Help yourself," Baxter said, pointing to the floor.

"Is it Jake Johnson's hair?" she asked. "Serina Smith said Sam sold her some."

"That little ferret," Dingdong said. She clearly thought hers had been an exclusive offer.

"Sorry," I said. "We're all out of Jake Johnson's hair. But we'll let you know next time he gets a haircut. See ya."

We were far too busy for time-wasters and the queue was getting restless.

"I heard there was a show while you waited," someone complained. "Animal tricks and stuff."

"And drinks," someone else joined in.

Now I could see why things had been going so smoothly. Sam had been running his own little business empire, keeping the crowds happy.

I made a mental note to make sure we got a share of his profits.

To be honest, I wished Sam was there right now. Then I looked up and saw him, hurtling towards us – on the end of his mum's arm. She had Clara, the baby, under the other one. I didn't know which was the scarier sight: Baxter's mum's face – which was fire-engine red – or Sam's hair – which was *bright purple*.

"Bill-yyy!" she was shouting.

When he heard his name, Baxter froze, scissors in mid snip. "Quick, scram," he said, tipping the boy whose hair he was cutting out of the chair.

At least *I* kept my business head on. "You still owe us two pounds fifty," I told the boy, as he made his escape. Well, he *had* had half a haircut!

"*Billy!*" his mum roared again. "This time you've gone too far!"

I pressed myself flat against the shed and tried to slide away, but she spotted me. "And you can stay where you are, Robin Banks."

She stopped in the shed doorway and slowly took in the baby bath, towels, scissors, hairdryer, mirror, magazines… "So this is where everything went," she said, amazed.

Fortunately for a moment words failed her. She just kept shaking her head and staring. But soon she was back in action, whizzing round the shed collecting up all her things, piling them into the baby bath.

"You've done some crazy things," she told Baxter. "But turning your brother's hair purple has got to be the craziest."

To be honest, she was wrong about that. This was only the craziest thing she knew about. Baxter's done far crazier things, believe me.

"Anyway, it's not *purple*," Baxter corrected her.

Even Sam was ready to defend his brother. It doesn't seem to matter what Baxter does to him, Sam's loyal to his last breath. "It's cool, Mum. Baxter says it's the latest colour, *Stewed Plum*."

"Stewed Plum! I'll *stew* the pair of you," she threatened.

She suddenly seemed to notice all the kids still waiting for haircuts, staring at her. "And you can all go home," she told them. "Just think yourselves lucky I came in time to save you from this." She held Sam out like a dire warning of what might have been.

"Actually, Auntie Carol," Dingdong spoke up, bravely, "Baxter's pretty good at it. I *like* what he did to mine. So do all the others."

"*All the others?*" Carol screeched. She struggled to calm herself down, then she said, very quietly, "I don't know how long it's been going on, but this little game is over. O-V-E-R. Understood?"

We all nodded and looked at the ground.

As she led Sam away she noticed the Happy Hair Saloon sign. "I'm surprised at you, Robin," she told me. "I thought *you* at least could spell better than that."

I didn't say a word; I knew when I'd got off lightly.

Baxter and me and Dingdong sat around the shed for the rest of the morning feeling very sorry for ourselves. But we felt even sorrier for Sam. We

could hear him getting his hair washed – over
and over again.

And then, as if things weren't bad enough,
Dingdong made her announcement: "Oh, well,
I'm going to be busy tomorrow anyway. Nigella's
coming for a sleepover."

Baxter and me looked at each other and
groaned. Talk about being trampled when we were
down. If the dreaded Horseface was going to be
hanging round the shed tomorrow, I thought,
I might just stay in bed – all day.

CHAPTER EIGHT

I wasn't joking. I seriously *meant* to stay in bed all day. But then I heard the dreaded sound of the hoover. I don't know about yours, but my mum's *always* bad-tempered when she hoovers. So I made a quick escape.

I found Baxter in the shed – back to destroying poor defenceless bits of wood. Sam was on the floor – you guessed it – messing with small furry animals. Apart from the sign still over the door, you'd have thought the Happy Hair Saloon never existed. It was back to no-business as usual.

At least the cash box was still full. I sat down and counted our money again. Eight-five pounds.

It was a real success story, but you know what bugged me? How close we'd been to making a hundred pounds. We'd have got there, too, if only Baxter's mum had come thundering in an hour later. What rotten timing.

"Dingdong's been round, asking for her share," Baxter told me. "But I didn't let her have it."

"She was fizzing mad," Sam said.

"The Medusa was with her," Baxter told me, as if I could have forgotten.

He sometimes calls Horseface 'The Medusa in disguise', but it's not much of a disguise, believe me.

What I don't understand is: Dingdong's OK, you know…for a girl. So how is it she can bear to hang out with someone who looks *and* sounds like a horse? Baxter says it's cos their mums are friends, but that's no excuse.

"Anyway, they've gone off shopping," Baxter added. "So we'll have a bit of peace."

Shopping, I thought. That's just like Dingdong, to want to blow our hard-earned money on hair bobbles or some other girly rubbish. But Baxter was no better. He was planning to spend his share on a flashlight and a new compass. No doubt Sam would buy more eye-wateringly smelly wildlife.

I seem to be the only one with any sense of forward planning.

"I think we should put the money into a new business," I suggested.

"What new business?" Baxter asked.

"That's the point. We need to come up with one," I said, "while we've got some money to invest in it."

Baxter looked doubtful. "Think we'd better wait till that's grown out," he nodded at Sam's still purple hair.

"After *five* hair washes," I said, "I'd have thought it would have already washed out."

"You mean *six*," Sam grumbled.

It seems Baxter had used *indelible* felt pens, so no wonder.

"How much did you make," I asked Sam, "with all your scams?"

"Five pounds fifty," he told me proudly.

"Well, hand it over," I said. "We'll put it in the pot."

Baxter said, "Leave it, Banksy. Don't you think he deserves it, after all he's been through."

"But we're so close to a hundred," I pleaded.

Baxter gave me a pitying look. Then *he* had the nerve to say to *me*, "Don't be so obsessive, Banksy."

I was too *flabbergasted* to reply.

We didn't get any further, because at that point Dingdong came back from the shops – with Horseface, or HF as I call her for short.

She walked up to the shed, looking down her horsey nose trying to find something to criticise. When she spotted the sign, she just about neighed herself silly.

"*Saloon*," she whinnied. "Which idiot wrote that?"

Baxter and me looked at each other and made

the cut throat sign. To be fair to Dingdong she tried to cover for Baxter. "It's like a joke, you know? A play on words?"

I thought that was pretty fast thinking on Dingdong's part.

But HF ignored her. "Yuk! Smells *vile* in here," she said. She pulled a face as if it was the most disgusting smell in the history of smells. I thought if she thinks *this* is smelly…

"Smelled fine till a minute ago," Baxter replied.

"Yeah," I agreed, "must be something the wind blew in."

HF pretended she hadn't heard that. "I can't believe you've been cutting people's hair in a *garden shed*," she said in genuine amazement.

"You'd better believe it," I said, rattling the cash box. "We've got the money to prove it."

"Bad luck," Baxter told her. "You missed a chance there to get a decent haircut for a change."

"For your information," she said, "I'm getting my hair done tomorrow – for *The Wedding*."

She made it sound like *The Royal Wedding*. Dingdong's face showed she'd heard more than enough about that particular event. Twenty minutes later so had we. If you've ever had a numb bum, you'll know how our brains felt.

Dingdong finally interrupted her, "Why don't you have it cut a bit shorter, like mine?"

HF turned and studied Dingdong for all of

half a second. "I don't think so," she said. "Not for a wedding."

"Well, everyone else likes it," Dingdong said. "Including Jake Johnson," she added, proudly.

This was news to us. HF suddenly paid attention. "*Really?*"

"When he was here on Monday, he said, 'Nice haircut, Dingdong.'"

"Jake Johnson was *here*?" Horseface *couldn't* believe that.

"Everyone from our class has been here," I told her, which wasn't that much of an exaggeration.

"Nearly all the girls have," Dingdong agreed.

Horseface hates being left out of anything. She suddenly began to look round the shed a little less critically now.

"Hmmm, well, in that case I suppose I *might* be interested."

"Oh, what a shame! You're too late," Baxter

jumped in. "We just closed for business."

I cut in quickly, "I'm sure we could fit in *one* last customer."

Baxter shook his head and drew a finger across his throat.

Dingdong looked doubtful as well. "I'm not sure that's such a good idea," she said.

"Why not?" HF turned on her. "I think you're jealous. I think you're worried I might get a better haircut than yours."

Dingdong narrowed her eyes. But before she could say anything else, I decided to close the deal. All I cared about was making that magic one hundred pounds.

"We'd do you a special price – as a friend of Dingdong's." I pretended to do tricky calculations in my head. "A final closing down offer of…twenty pounds. What do you say?"

HF breathed in. She looked Dingdong's haircut

over once more and then said, "Fifteen, and not a penny more."

"Done," I said. "You drive a hard bargain, Nigella."

"Yes, I know," she said, smugly. "And I shall expect my money's worth."

"Oh, you'll get it," I promised her. "Every penny of it."

CHAPTER NINE

Baxter was glaring at me as if I'd made a deal with the devil – and he was the sacrifice.

"I'm *not* doing it," he mouthed at me. But I pretended I couldn't tell what he was on about.

"Well, if we're going to do it," Horseface announced, "there are a few things we'll need to get straight. First, I want all these animals outside. Every last one of them! And the floor brushed. I'm not having my hair washed with a hosepipe, you can forget that. And I shall need a mirror, so I can keep my eye on you."

Baxter almost erupted, but before he could say anything, Dingdong took charge.

"I've got an idea," she said. "We'll go and have lunch at my house. We can wash your hair there, while the boys are getting the place ready. Come on, Nigella."

As they left, Dingdong turned and gave me a look that let me know she'd had enough of Horseface, too, and her boring wedding. And whatever happened now, she was definitely on our team.

But, unfortunately, the minute they'd gone the rest of our team revolted.

"Forget it, Banksy," Baxter exploded. "I'm not doing it."

"And I'm not moving the cages," Sam whined. "I only just got them all back inside."

They were both going to take a lot of persuading, especially Baxter. I should probably explain the background between him and HF.

Nigella Horseforth only joined our school about a year ago. Before that she went to some posh place she's always going on about. She's one of those people who's dead clever, but stupid at the same time. You know? She always comes top in tests and homework, but she's an idiot out of the classroom. Baxter's sort of the opposite: he can't spell or do maths and his handwriting sometimes looks like a demented spider has been let loose on the page. But in every other way, Baxter's so sharp he could cut himself.

At school, though, HorseFace never misses a chance to make him look stupid. You can hear that horsey laugh of hers every time he gets something wrong.

Even worse, she's the biggest snitch in the world.

There was one time Baxter did this really crazy

cartoon of our teacher. The whole class loved it. But HF said, "Let's see how funny Miss Waites thinks that is, shall we?"

Miss Waites didn't think it was funny *at all.* Baxter missed football for a whole month. He has never forgiven her.

I took a deep breath and swivelled Baxter's chair round until he faced me.

"Look, Baxter, I understand," I told him. "I really do. But think how good you'll feel when we've made a hundred pounds."

"You mean how good *you'll* feel," he replied.

"We're a team," I reminded him. "Do it for the team."

Baxter looked at me pityingly.

"Well, then, do it for me," I begged.

But it was hopeless; I needed a new approach. I needed to play on his vanity.

"OK, better quit while you're winning," I said. "You're probably right. Not even you could make Horseface look less like a horse."

Baxter took the bait and swallowed it whole. "Listen," he told me. "With my skills, I could make even *her* look good."

"Does that mean you'll do it?" I asked, holding my breath.

Baxter still looked doubtful. "If my mum finds

out I'll be hung, drawn, quartered and then fed to the dogs."

"She doesn't ever need to know," I said.

"Anyway she's taken all our gear," he reminded me.

"I'll get scissors, a towel, whatever you need," I offered.

I could see he was *almost* persuaded.

"But there's no way I'm letting her lay down all the rules," Baxter insisted.

He absolutely drew the line at the mirror. So we came to a compromise. We sent Sam to *borrow* his mum's mirror again, but we covered it this time with one of my mum's scarves.

I dashed around organising everything else, borrowing my mum's scissors, a towel, a hairdryer. Lucky for me she was at work. Then I helped Sam carry all the cages back outside.

"And make sure you keep Rooney out of the

way," I told him. "For the next hour at least."

After that I brushed out the shed. Well, I gave it what Mum calls a lick and a promise – just enough to keep HF quiet.

Baxter was sitting all this time trying to persuade himself he was up to the challenge. "I can do this," he said to no one in particular. "I'm not afraid of her. I'm *Mister Luigi*."

"That's right," I told him. "You *can* do it." Then I kept my fingers tightly crossed and prayed that he could.

Just then the girls came back; HF was still yakking about weddings.

"Did I tell you my bridesmaid's dress is costing *two hundred and fifty pounds*?"

"Only twenty times," Dingdong muttered. She looked like one more mention of the 'W' word and she'd cut HF's head off, never mind her hair.

HF had a big white towel wrapped round her head like a turban. She glanced around, sniffily, then sat in Baxter's swivel chair. She looked like the Queen settling herself on her throne.

"It's a *bit* better," she sniffed, looking down her long nose at everything. "And I suppose *for a shed* it's as good as it's going to get."

Baxter closed his eyes and counted to ten.

"Steady," I whispered.

I handed Baxter my mum's scissors. He pushed up his sleeves and took them – like a surgeon preparing to operate. "Ready?" he asked HF.

"I really must be crazy," she whinnied, taking off the towel. "Luckily you don't have to be able to read or write to cut hair," she sniggered. Then she dealt the final blow. "Still, I suppose it's not your fault you can't, living in a place like this."

Oh, woah! Now she'd finally pushed Baxter too far. I recognised that evil glint in his eye. He looked like Sweeny Todd, the demon barber again. I could see all was lost.

He turned to me, scissors at the ready. I knew what he wanted: my permission to get his revenge.

Even Dingdong was nodding, so I nodded too. "Just remember," I told him, "Nigella wants her money's worth."

And that was all the encouragement Baxter needed.

CHAPTER TEN

Before I tell you what happened next, I want you to imagine yourself in Baxter's place. Could you resist that kind of temptation? Honestly? No, nor me.

So, I suddenly thought, I'd better get her money off her first, before the hair hits the floor.

"I've never heard of having to pay *before* you get your hair cut," she grumbled.

"Well, it's the way we do business," I told her, firmly.

I pocketed the fifteen pounds and could hardly

stop myself from grinning. We'd done it; we'd made o*ne hundred pounds*! I felt like cheering, but somehow managed to control myself.

Baxter made a start towelling HF's hair dry, rather roughly, I thought. And he didn't use the white towel I'd brought. He used a grubby brown one his mum dried the dogs on.

"Excuse *me*," HF said, snapping her head back.

"Try not to do that," Baxter said, very calmly, as he eased her head forward again. "I wouldn't want to cut you…by mistake."

He yanked the comb through her hair without mercy. And when she complained he said, "Oh, sorry," then did it all over again. Amazingly, she seemed to put up with it.

Finally he was ready to cut. I thought he'd just grab handfuls and saw away, but he didn't. Instead, he hardly cut some sections at all. But others he cut almost up to her ears. Baxter hummed all the

while, as if he was really enjoying his work. HF kept trying to get a sly look, but since we'd covered the mirror she gave up and closed her eyes.

I felt like closing mine, but I didn't. It was like watching *Dr Who* when I was little. I couldn't bear to miss it but it was almost too scary to watch. Something pretty bad was about to happen, but it was out of my hands. And, anyway, I reminded myself, she *did* deserve it.

"Hang on in there. Nearly finished," Baxter told her. "You're doing really well." He sounded like a dentist trying to reassure someone before he goes in with the drill.

It was at this point I noticed Sam had brought Rooney in, even though I'd told him not to. Dingdong and Sam were putting their heads together about something.

Out of the blue, Dingdong suddenly asked Horseface if she wanted some crisps. She said she didn't, but Dingdong insisted on putting some in her lap – *for later*.

By now Baxter was almost finished. HF demanded to see it. But he told her, "Two more minutes. Just got to blow it dry."

Dingdong stepped forward nervously, holding the hairdryer, but Baxter said, "Don't worry, I'm going to finish this one off."

He yanked each section of hair and pulled it as tight as he could. "This might feel a bit *firm*," he told HF, "but it's the very latest way of straightening hair. Well worth the pain."

Although HF grumbled and complained to

herself, she put up with it all pretty bravely,
I thought.

When Baxter stood back, the finished effect
was *mind-blowing*! Dingdong's hair had a bit of
a wavy bottom, like a merry-go-round. But HF's
looked like the battlements of a castle. It made
me think of a word we'd learned in history –
crenellated.

Uh oh, I thought, any minute now she's going
to be storming Baxter's battlements. But Baxter
seemed to be keeping his nerve amazingly well.
"All done," he said.

He nodded to Sam to move the scarf to let
Horseface see the finished effect.

When she looked into the mirror she saw
her own reflection, which would have been bad
enough. But, at the very same moment, she saw
Sam – with a large white rat on his shoulder. And
Rooney was looking straight at *her*.

It wasn't really *her* he had his eye on, or to be more accurate his *nose*. It was the chocolate and chilli flavoured crisps that Dingdong had kindly left in her lap.

The rat suddenly made a spectacular leap off Sam's shoulder and landed smack in the middle of the crisps on Nigella's knee.

I should think they heard her screams in every hair salon in Manchester. The last we saw of HF she was racing and screaming into the far distance.

But not before I'd had the presence of mind
to whip out my phone and catch it all on camera.
Snap! Snap!

Team GRQ did a four-way high-five. Of course
we knew that very soon the *doodoo* would hit the
fan. But for now we were going to enjoy every
moment of our success.

Have you ever thought that sometimes *even
big trouble* is completely worth it? Well, let me
tell you, this was one of those times.

Of course, we did pay for it in the end. The next
day, in fact, the bubble burst when Dingdong
came and told us HF's parents were thinking of
suing us!

"*Suing us?*" I said, panicked. I knew we should
have taken out insurance.

Luckily, in the end, Dingdong's mum
persuaded them to settle for her money back.

There goes our record, I thought sadly.

But Dingdong hadn't finished. "As well as…"

"As well as what?" I asked.

"The price of a professional hairdresser to put it all right."

We shrugged. It's not like we had a lot of choice.

But Dingdong still hadn't finished. "That's if we can afford it."

"What do you mean?" I asked.

"They're taking her to a top salon in the city. It's going to cost…" she paused for dramatic effect. "Eighty pounds."

"*Eighty pounds!*" I almost screamed.

"Apparently it's what these places charge," Dingdong told us.

"You mean to tell me," Baxter said gobsmacked, "*we* could have been charging eighty pounds a time?"

"No, Dumbo. These are top professionals." Dingdong said.

Even so, I agreed with Baxter – we'd obviously been underselling ourselves.

Baxter was all for blackmailing Horseface with the photos, but I agreed with Dingdong, she'd paid enough.

"We'll keep them, though," I said. "In case we ever need to put her in her place again."

Once we'd paid off Horseface we'd made a grand profit of *five pounds*! It was less than Sam had made with his animal tricks and locks of Jake Johnson's hair. I felt gutted.

We all sat around for the rest of the afternoon at a bit of a loose end. It was the last day of half term.

Baxter was trimming the end of his frayed rope with a pair of nail scissors. He had one of those crazy looks he sometimes gets as he snipped the air.

"What about a final haircut?" he said, looking straight at me.

No way, José.

The only other time I've seen Baxter looking this dangerous was in his mad Masterchef phase.

Remind me next time to tell you all about that.

Now that really was completely OTT.

Seriously, if you think this story takes some believing, wait till you hear that one.